When Death Becomes Her

Kim Evans

This is a work of fiction. Names, characters, places and incidents are the product of the author's imagination or used fictitiously. Any resemblance to actual persons, living or dead, events or locales is entirely coincidental.

Copyright © 2024 Kim Evans

All rights reserved. No part of this book may be reproduced or used in any manner without the prior written permission of the copyright owner, except for the use of brief quotations in a book review.

To request permissions, contact the publisher at kim306@btinternet.com

Paperback: ISBN 9798339148593

First paperback edition October 2024.

Author Kim Evans

Editor Jodie L Evans

Cover art by Jodie L Evans

Dedicated to my mam, Eliza, who passed away during the time I was writing this book. Forever in my heart, with my dad. Her name now forever in my book.

Clara

Prologue

Clara's favourite painting once hung in the farmhouse that she shared with her husband, Jack. The painting showed a family at the beach, carefree and happy, playing with a beach ball on golden sand that trailed off into a tranquil deep blue sea. Clara had this odd feeling that the painting was always meant to be hers somehow.

Clara was happy once, when she was a young bride looking forward to what she believed would be a long and happy life with Jack. She loved how he looked at her like she was the only person in the world. She always felt truly adored by him. All of that smashed like a vase on concrete when she caught Jack in their bed with the housemaid. Clara couldn't speak. She heard Jack running out into the hallway, calling her name, but she fled as quickly as she could, not once looking back. Clara's whole life changed in one split second, leaving her heart beyond repair.

The painting had been displayed on the wall in their stairway, next to a portrait that Jack had commissioned of Clara for their first wedding anniversary. He told her she looked breathtaking in it, but now all of those words he once said to her had become meaningless. For her portrait, she wore a dark maroon, long-sleeved dress with a small matching hat and matching lipstick. She wore her black hair mostly down to show off the waves that reached the middle of her back, with just a little of it pinned up to keep it out of her face. Everyone commented on it and said she looked beautiful that day, but she didn't think it portrayed the real her. She was never comfortable in those fancy gowns. She was happy that day because her husband looked at her like she was the most beautiful woman in the world. She was blissfully unaware that her life wasn't as rosy as she thought it was.

Jack didn't even bother looking for her after she left; he stayed with his mistress. Clara had all the answers she needed about whether or not he really loved her. Her heart didn't just break; it shattered into tiny shards, so small that she would never be able to put them all back together. The Clara she used to be no longer existed; she was completely lost. She gave away the baby she was carrying, unable to live with any reminders of her life with Jack. She couldn't bear being reminded every day of how much of a fool she'd been and how she had been betrayed. The baby girl went to live with a young couple who were unable to have children of their own, and Clara knew she would have a better life with them than Clara could ever give her.

She lived a short life, her body consumed with bitterness and rage and hatred for the world and everyone in it. She couldn't stand to see anyone else happy or at peace. She spent her last few years wishing she could pour all the poison that had built up in her mind onto others. A woman in the town where Clara shopped experimented with spells and taught Clara how to place curses. She said Clara had the perfect dark aura about her to make it work, and by that time, Clara had become so hardened that she believed that was the person she was meant to be. She knew the perfect object for it, too. When she left the farm, her parents went back to retrieve her belongings, including her beloved beach painting.

As she took the last few breaths of her unhappy life, she placed a curse on it.

After she passed, her spirit became imbedded within the painting, and she travelled around with it to different places and different homes, manipulating the people around her and watching it all play out until eventually someone's life was taken. Then her work was done, and she would move on elsewhere.

It surprised Clara how many people have secrets. She played the people involved like puppets, planting doubts and revealing things they would otherwise never know. She vowed that somebody would die every time. Someone so loved that the people they left behind would be completely devastated. She enjoyed the thrill of it all. She felt like her life had been wasted. She wished she had been able to move on, but she never could.

The first owners of the painting, Charles and Emma, were a complicated couple. Clara hadn't realised how messy some people's lives could be, even without her help.

Emma & Charles

It's been weeks since Emma last walked down the magnificent staircase that cascades like a waterfall into their hallway or opened the front door and caught that first breath of fresh air. She tries to picture the front garden, its carpet of deep green grass spreading across acres, the kaleidoscope of flowers running around the edges of it. She wonders if her husband, Charles, is keeping up with the maintenance, if it's still as beautiful, and if she'll ever see it again.

She can't see anything from her bedroom window since Charles boarded it up, insisting it was the doctor's orders to keep bright lights out of the bedroom. This would increase Emma's chances of recovering from the mysterious illness that had crept up on her body. The doctor, who has been a good friend of Charles's for decades, said she had to stay in bed until she could regain her strength. Charles also tries to convince her that it's for her own good that the door always remains locked and that she's always served bland, tasteless food, but it's all starting to feel like some kind of punishment.

Charles doesn't think Emma's noticed that she always feels nauseous and dizzy each time she takes the pill he gives her every evening. Her husband is poisoning her and has been, very slowly, for a while now. She's felt herself become weaker and weaker as the weeks have passed. Or had done, until recently. After weeks of standing over her, ensuring each pill was swallowed, it seems Charles has become too complacent with their new routine. He barely sticks around anymore, giving Emma the opportunity to slip the pills beneath her pillow until she can hide them somewhere better later on.

Six months ago, Charles's cousin, Louise, introduced them both to a friend of hers named Lisa. She started bringing her to the house, and Emma quickly became suspicious that Lisa and her husband had begun, or would begin, having an affair. Lisa made no secret of her feelings towards Charles, openly flirting with him in front of Emma, always flicking and twirling her long blonde curly hair, and giggling at his awful jokes like some love-struck teenager. Lisa was very beautiful, and Charles was obviously taken with her immediately. Soon enough, Lisa was visiting their home without Louise to accompany her, and she and Charles began playing tennis in their private courts next to the garden, away from the prying eyes of Emma.

Emma realised Charles had probably chosen tennis because he knew Emma didn't like it, so she was unlikely to join them. Emma preferred to walk around the garden or sit out there on a blanket with a book. It was her favourite place, like something out of a fairy tale. She thought she could get lost in them forever and she wouldn't even mind. Emma started to care less and less each time Lisa's shrill laughter echoed over to her from the tennis court while she read in the garden. What was once her place of peaceful solitude was now tainted by the sounds of another woman having fun with her husband.

When Charles became all about work, Emma's love for him had started to diminish. It was hard to love someone who only cared about work above everything else. At least, that's how he was until Lisa came along. Now he was behaving like the old Charles, but with someone else. He was never really a romantic guy, but Emma had found him fun to be around at first. It's hard to imagine now, but he used to make her laugh a lot. They had good times together in the first few years, but the good times became less frequent after their children, Marian and Charlie, came along. They're both adults now, with their own lives.

It was easier for Emma when her dad was still around because Charles would never risk doing anything that might upset him. Her father worked hard in real estate, leaving her a large sum of money when he passed, which paid for the extravagant mansion they now call home. Emma's father hired Charles when they got engaged, and Charles has continued to run the business now that he's gone. The business is in Emma's name though. She can't imagine Charles would ever want to divorce or separate from her because he would never want to give that up, but she was determined not to let him make a fool of her.

When he returned from his tennis session with Lisa one day, she snapped and laid everything out for him.

'If you insist on continuing this little thing you've got going with Lisa, I will divorce you. Don't even try to deny it; I am neither blind nor stupid. It's your choice. I don't want to see her around here again.'

He didn't try to deny it. He hesitated for a moment, like he wanted to say something, but then thought better of it and continued on his way up the stairs. She assumed he would just ignore her threat and carry on anyway, maybe try to be a bit more discrete about it, but things took a darker turn than she could ever have imagined.

It was the following week when she began to feel ill. She was sick every day and could barely stand without support. At first, the doctor said it was probably some kind of flu and it would get better with rest, but it didn't.

*

When Emma became ill, the sickness got worse every day, until all she wanted to do was lay down all the time. It was the only thing that helped with the nausea and dizziness. After a couple of weeks, she noticed how she started to feel a little better in the late afternoon, until evening came and she took her pill from Charles. Then it would start all over again. That's when she started to suspect Charles. She tried to brush off her suspicions at first, thinking she was being foolish and that maybe the illness was making her lose her mind. How could she think her husband would do such a thing? What reason would he have for it?

But she couldn't shake her suspicions. It was impossible in the beginning to refuse the pills with Charles standing over her, watching, making sure she swallowed them. Spending that much time with her must have become too much of a chore for him, though, as he started just handing the pills to her and leaving. She seized the opportunity to test her theory, and soon she could feel the difference in her body on the days she didn't take them. She started doing little exercises when Charles wasn't around, just little things like walking around the bedroom. It isn't much, but it's a start, something to help her regain a little strength. She exercises her arms by brushing her hair, counting the strokes each night, doing more and more the stronger she gets. She can't let Charles find out about this though. That's another good thing about these old, large homes; there's always a creaky floorboard or two to let you know when someone is near.

Charles's cousin, Louise, visits more frequently now that Emma doesn't seem to be recovering and spends all day every day locked up in the dark bedroom. Emma can never tell her about Charles, but she has a feeling Louise is becoming suspicious too. Emma knows she didn't bring Lisa here with the intention of her causing trouble in their marriage. In fact, when Emma confided in her about their affair, Louise cut off all contact with Lisa. Emma and Louise have always gotten along well, but Emma knows she can't risk telling anyone what's going on until she's able to get away from Charles.

She spends most of the day in bed with a book, straining her eyes to focus on the words by the only dim lamp Charles allows her to keep by her bed. Books have been her saviour through all this, keeping her mind occupied during the long, quiet days. In the afternoon, she takes another walk around the bedroom. She's usually left completely alone most of the afternoon anyway. She wonders if Lisa still comes around, but it's not worth asking Charles. He would deny it anyway, and she doesn't want to antagonise him further.

Molly will pop in soon to help Emma with anything she needs and to take her washing away. Molly used to work for Emma's father, and Emma employed her immediately after his death. She's loyal and has always taken good care of Emma, but she can't tell her either, for fear of what Charles might do to her. Emma's just glad for her company on the short visits she makes to her room throughout the day.

As Emma looks around the once bright and grand bedroom, it makes her sad to see it so dark and gloomy. It used to be so beautiful in the light, but now it's as though the room has taken on the burden of her misery. The golden edges around her dressing table, mirror, wardrobe, and headboard used to flicker with reflections of sunlight. Now, you can barely even see that they're gold. She misses the curtains being drawn back in the morning and all the light pouring into the room, like the room was waking up from a deep sleep too, all fresh and bright and ready for the day. All her little trinkets, ornaments, and her jewellery box would glimmer like a mini carousel of treasures.

There's a painting hanging above the bed, showing a family at the seaside, playing happily with a beach ball. Charles bought it for Emma one year for her birthday. Emma had been captivated by it at first glance. There was something so fascinating, almost haunting, about it, though Emma could never quite put her finger on what it was. There were stories at the store where he bought it about it being cursed. Even after they had been told that, Emma found it impossible to leave behind. She had thought about getting rid of it many times, but she couldn't quite let go of it, despite it being a gift from Charles.

Molly stirs Emma from her thoughts and arrives to help her wash. Emma could probably do it herself, but that's her little secret for now.

'Hello, Miss. How are you feeling today?' Molly asks, always with genuine concern.

'Just a little tired and weak. I didn't get a lot of sleep last night.'

'Get some today then, Miss. It'll do you good.' Molly leans back a little to inspect Emma's face. 'You do have a little more colour in your cheeks lately.'

'Do you think so?' Emma asks, trying to hide her worry that people will start to notice she's getting better. She'll have to start applying some powder to her face to cover that up.

'Yes, I think maybe you could be on the mend one day soon. That'll be lovely, won't it, Miss? You can get back outside then and enjoy some long overdue fresh air.'

'I hope so, Molly, but I do think it could be a while yet.'

'Of course, dear. We won't rush you. You'll have to be much stronger than you are now, but don't worry, you'll get there.' She places a reassuring hand on Emma's arm, smiling kindly at her. Emma wishes she could tell her the truth.

'Will Marian and Charlie be calling in this week, Miss?'

Neither of the children have any idea what's going on; they just think their mother is extremely ill and remain hopeful that she'll recover one day if she follows the doctor's advice.

'Yes, they're coming tomorrow,' Emma replies. She always looks forward to her children visiting. She says children, but they're adults now. No matter how grown up they are, though, they'll always be her babies. She wants to be able to spend more time with them, but Charles keeps putting it in their heads that their visits are too much for Emma and that they wear her out. That's why they only visit once a week for now.

'Does Charles have many visitors to the house? Apart from the children and Ella?' Emma asks Molly.

'Not really, Miss. Some of his business associates sometimes. They usually just ask for some tea and go into his office for a while. I imagine it's all work talk, boring stuff that you wouldn't be interested in anyway, Miss.'

'No female callers? Lisa?'

Molly avoids Emma's eyes and fusses over the washing.

'No, Miss. Well, maybe she's popped in a few times, but don't think about silly little things like that.' She pauses and looks at her seriously now. 'I'm here to look after you, Miss. Don't you worry about that.'

'I know, Molly, and I'm so grateful to you. I'll never forget everything you've done for me.'

'Well, don't go talking like you're leaving us anytime soon. You'll get well again; I know you will. You're strong, strong up here,' she says, pointing to her head.

She gives Emma a hug. She's the only one who does these days, apart from the children.

'I'll leave you in peace to get some rest now, Miss.'

Most maids call a married woman Madam, but Molly has been with Emma's family since Emma was a young girl, so she's always called her Miss, and Emma wouldn't have it any other way.

*

According to the clock next to her bed, it's almost time to sleep again. The days and nights continue to blend into each other in this dark room, void of all daylight. Emma is sitting in front of her mirror, brushing her hair after a few slow laps of walking around the room. She only manages ten brush strokes with her left arm, but twenty with her right, and has to take her time or she'll lose her strength. Her hair is thinner than it used to be, and she doesn't think it's because she's getting older, like Charles insists. It's because of what he's doing to her. Her long, dark hair used to be so thick and strong. She hopes it can be again one day. Charles tried to convince her to let someone cut it for her, but she refused. He's not taking that away from her too.

The beautiful golden brush Emma uses belonged to her mother. Her dad had put a few things away after her mother died and gave them to Emma when she was older. Emma was only six when her mother died from a brief but devastating illness that just arrived one day like an uninvited and unwanted guest. It ravished her quickly. Emma's father was devastated, leaving Emma worried that he might end up sending her away. She was afraid he wouldn't be capable of looking after her in his heartbroken state, but he did. In time, he realised how much Emma had lost too and stopped trying to distract himself by working so many hours. They worked through their grief and healed together. He never remarried. Emma thinks it was because he couldn't stand the thought of losing someone like that again. The grief consumed him for a long time. Years later, he told her that if it hadn't been for her, he probably would have given up, let his grief consume him, and given in to his broken heart. He told Emma he was so grateful for the time he had with her mother and hoped that Emma would be lucky enough to find the same kind of love herself one day.

'Don't settle for anything less than your true love,' he had told her.

She had thought once that Charles was her true love but realised a few years later that she was wrong. It was too late by then, of course. They were married, and their first child, Marian, had been born.

Emma believes her true love came later, and she has

already lost him now. John used to work for Emma and Charles as their gardener. Emma spent so much time in the garden, it wasn't too long before a friendship blossomed between them. John was kind, funny, and always took great pride in his work. Emma enjoyed talking to him while he worked, and he often took an interest in the books she was reading. Sometimes they would sit on the bench together, drinking lemonade while he took his break. She started to enjoy spending time with him more than she enjoyed spending time with her husband, but she knew it was wrong, so she tried to ignore her feelings for him. She stopped frequenting the garden so often when he was working, even though she desperately wanted to speak to him. One day, he didn't turn up for work. When Emma asked Charles if he had heard from John, Charles said that John had left to take care of a sick relative. Emma never saw or heard from him again. She was heartbroken. That's when she realised John was the love of her life. She couldn't tell anyone about it, so she was forced to grieve in solitude. As some time passed, she got used to the nauseating feeling in the pit of her stomach, which has eased over time but never completely gone. Emma thought maybe Molly knew how she felt about John, but she never brought it up. Nothing would ever have come of it anyway. Emma knows she would have stayed loyal to Charles, which is the main reason she was so upset over his affair with Lisa. She had sacrificed her happiness to be a loyal wife, but Charles didn't seem to care at all about his loyalty to Emma.

A creaking floorboard outside alerts her to someone heading towards her bedroom. Emma makes it to the bed as quick as she can, putting her feet up and trying to calm her breathing so it doesn't look like she's been out of bed. She takes slow, deep breaths until the door opens and Charles walks in.

'How are you feeling?' he asks indifferently, looking around the room instead of at her.

'I'm tired and weak as usual,' she says, with her head rested back against her pillow. 'Have you ever considered that some fresh air might help me? I'd love to see the garden again. You could take me in my wheelchair, or Molly could?'

He glares at her now and scoffs at her suggestion.

'Has Molly been putting silly suggestions into your head? You know what the doctor said about the light.'

'No, it was my idea,' Emma replies. 'I miss the garden and the flowers. I really think it could help me. Isn't it worth a try? If it doesn't work, then there's no harm done, right?'

'Wrong. It's not going to happen, dear. You can forget about that for now.'

Emma begins to feel desperate.

'But I'm going crazy stuck in here all the time. How about just downstairs in the sitting room for an hour some time?'

Charles sighs, softens his eyes and his voice, and moves a little closer to Emma.

'Look, I know I've been neglecting you lately because I've been busy with work. How about next week I get the chef to make us a nice meal and we can get a table brought in here so we can eat together? I'll get a big, bright lamp brought in too.' He looks around the room as though he's only realising now how dark it really is. There's no regret in his expression, though.

'That sounds nice,' Emma says. 'Could we have a traditional roast dinner, like my mother used to make? Maybe even a rich fruit cake for dessert?'

'You can have whatever you want, dear,' he says, turning and leaving the room with a smug grin on his face, leaving Emma worrying what her husband is planning for her.

*

* * *

Charles wants to put an end to this now. He really thought Emma would have succumbed to the effects of the pills by now. Either she's stronger than he thought or the pills are just not up to the job. His only concern is how much the children will miss her, but he puts all the blame on Emma. She started this when she began eyeing up the help. How stupid did she think he was? Did she really think he hadn't noticed their lingering glances, their conversations over lemonade in the garden? It was only a matter of time before they were at it behind his back.

Afterwards, he wondered if she really did have feelings for the gardener or if it was just a physical attraction. She never bothered trying to find him after he left. Either way, he wasn't letting her leave him so that she could share her wealth with a nobody like John.

Charles will inherit Emma's money, then he can marry Lisa, and they can enjoy their new life together. The kids will be fine; they have their own lives now. Marian has a good husband and works in a library, which she loves. Charlie travels a lot, enjoying his youth before he thinks about settling down and starting a family of his own. Charles tries to convince himself that they might not even miss Emma that much. She's hardly been much of a mother to them the last few months, and they've always been very independent. Emma wanted them to be that way, so they could always be in charge of their own lives, not have it dictated to them by others.

Charles wonders if he'll feel any guilt or remorse when Emma's gone, but he doesn't believe he will. As beautiful as she is, he doesn't think she ever really loved him, not truly, not like you're supposed to love your husband. He thinks they both rushed into their marriage. He's not quite sure what Emma's reasons were; she probably can't remember either. Charles didn't really give her much of a chance to change her mind anyway. He had his eyes on the money from the beginning and was determined to be her husband one way or another.

Lisa isn't like Emma. She's young and full of life. She doesn't take life too seriously; she just wants to have fun. Charles hopes that doesn't change when they get married. She always seems so eager to please him, so he can't see that happening. He's already told her he doesn't want more children, so that's out in the open and won't be an issue. Having children would change her, like it changed Emma. When Emma had someone else to take care of and give her love and attention to, Charles became a blur in the background. Emma blames him, of course, for not wanting to be more involved with the children, but Charles's believed that wasn't his job, it was hers. Emma told him that she had to give them so much attention to make up for his lack of interest. Charles won't make the same mistake with Lisa; children won't be an issue.

He knew Emma knew about him and Lisa. It's not like Lisa had been subtle about it. Charles wasn't exactly doing his best to hide it either. He wishes he'd tried harder to keep it a secret, but the damage is done now and there's no going back.

*

Lisa can't quite comprehend how much of a fool Charles is. He really does think she's head over heels for him. She is a very good actress though; it is her job after all. She loves the drama and theatrics of performing on stage. This job was different though, the role of being a seducer. She had been hired to lure some desperate middle-aged man into an affair, all the while keeping an eye on his wife. She found Charles to be dull, but she loved spending time at their mansion, the grandeur of being there, playing tennis on their private court.

She felt guilty around Emma, though she never showed it. Everyone apart from Charles spoke so highly of Emma, and Lisa knew she didn't deserve what she was doing to her, but she'd been told by her employer that it was all for Emma's own good. Lisa does feel some kind of redemption since Charles confided in her about his plans to poison Emma so they can have the house and money all to themselves. He said it would need to be done slowly to avoid suspicion. He would make it seem as though she was ill for months before her death, so no one would ask any questions.

Lisa took this information back to her employer, who gave her sedatives to swap with the pills Charles was giving to Emma. They would keep her feeling groggy without putting her in any danger. It worked. Charles thinks the pills are working as they should.

Lisa thinks of Emma often, wondering how she's doing locked in that bedroom alone. Charles lets Lisa in on his plan to end things, with a final meal with his wife in her room, a glass of wine to follow, and the final pills. He wants Lisa to be waiting downstairs for him, like an instant replacement. She will be there, but not to be a waiting trophy for Charles. She'll be there to switch the glasses over.

*

Emma's stomach has been doing cartwheels at the thought of what Charles has planned for their special meal. She had a feeling he was getting impatient, and now it seems he's had enough and wants to finish her off for good. It has to be that. She knows he doesn't actually want to spend time with her, not now after everything that's happened.

Does she just accept her fate, or should she fight it? She

doesn't know how to fight it with her body being so weak. If it hadn't been for her visits from Molly and the kids and having her books to read, she probably would have given up months ago.

Emma hears the familiar creaks of movement outside her bedroom. She's delighted to see that it's Marian and Charlie. Her mood lifts immediately upon seeing their faces, and it reminds her that she has a reason to fight.

'Hi Mum, you look a little better today,' Marian says with a kind smile. 'You have some colour in your cheeks again.'

'She's right, you do,' Charlie agrees.

They both take a seat, seeming hopeful that their mother's health is improving.

'I would love to get outside soon,' says Emma. 'Get some of that clean, fresh air in my lungs, see the beautiful garden.'

'Would you like me to ask Dad if we could take you today?' asks Charlie. 'I'm sure…'

'Not today,' Marian interrupts. 'Maybe next week? I think you're still too weak for that at the moment, sorry. I'd like to see you a bit stronger first.'

'That's okay,' says Emma. 'Honestly, you're probably right. It was just a thought.'

'I'll talk to Dad next time,' says Charlie, wanting to leave Emma with some hope of being able to leave this room soon. 'I think it might do you some good to get out of this dark, dreary room. I still don't understand why you need to be locked in here. Every time I bring it up, Dad just yells about respecting the doctor's advice. I hope Dad's looking after you.'

'It won't be for much longer, darling,' says Emma reassuringly. 'As you said, I'm getting some colour back and I have been feeling a bit stronger this week.'

'If you say so, but I'm coming to see you twice a week from now on. Dad can't stop me,' says Charlie defiantly.

'Me too,' says Marian.

They all hug, and Emma wonders if this will be the last time she'll ever see them. She watches them chatting away, not really listening to anything they're saying, just trying to take in every inch of their faces, watching them smile and knowing they're happy.

Not long after they leave, Charles enters her bedroom.

'The kids want to visit you on Thursday every week now, as well as Sunday,' he says. 'Is that your doing?'

'No, it was their idea, but what if it had been mine? So what? They're my kids. Of course I want to see them as often as I can. Why would you have a problem with that, Charles?'

'I don't have a problem with it. I was just curious. Anyway, it'll be nice for you to see them more often. I'll have to watch I don't keep you up too late for our meal on Wednesday.'

'Wednesday?' she says, almost choking on the word.

'Yes, do you have any other plans?' he asks sarcastically. 'I've told the chef to prepare the dinner that you requested, along with the dessert you requested. It's all arranged.'

Emma tries to keep her face calm, but Charles must register the fear or worry in her eyes.

'You seemed happy about it yesterday. Has something changed? Do you not want a meal with your husband?'

'Of course I do. You could have had dinner in here with me any time, but you chose not to.'

'You weren't up to it then, dear. You seem to be a bit better now. So, Wednesday it is.'

She catches the smirk on his face as he turns towards the door to leave, turning the key in the lock behind him yet again. Emma's stomach twists and turns at the thought of how things have turned out. She tries to distract herself by going over to her dressing table to brush her hair. She needs all the strength she can get now. She's considering asking Molly for help. As much as she doesn't want to get her involved, she doesn't see how she can possibly fight this by herself.

When Molly comes in to help her get ready to settle down for the night, Emma can't take it any longer. She breaks down into tears and tells Molly everything, all about what Charles has been doing and what she suspects he's going to do next. Molly is too stunned to speak for a while.

'I'm so sorry, Miss.' She stumbles over her words. 'I should have seen this. How did I not see this? I mean, I had some small suspicions about how Charles was treating you, but nothing on this level. You seemed so ill, and the doctor seemed to think so too, so I just believed it all.'

'Charles has been very clever about it all, Molly. You weren't to know. He even has the kids fooled, although Charlie has started asking questions. I couldn't tell them though. I'm not sure anymore what he's actually capable of. That's why I didn't want to tell you. I just really didn't know what else to do.'

'So you think he's going to put something in your food? Or your drink?'

'I think he'll probably go for the drink. It'll be easier for him to do that without being seen. The chef never lets anyone near the food.'

'What if I switch them, Miss? The drinks? You won't get a chance to, but I'll probably have to bring the trolley up anyway. He'd have to do it before he comes into your room, wouldn't he?'

'You would do that for me, Molly?'

'Of course I would, Miss. You're like a daughter to me. I love you, dear,' she says, leaning over and kissing Emma's forehead gently. 'I won't let Charles get away with this.'

For the first time in a long time, Emma feels safe.

*

* * *

Lisa has to put on her best performance yet when Charles tells her all about his arrangements for Wednesday evening. He calls it his 'last supper' with Emma, with such an evil grin on his face that Lisa wants to slap it clean off. But she can't. He tells her that the plan is to put a load of the pills he's been giving Emma into her glass of wine, and Lisa realises that the amount he's planning, even with the sedatives, will likely be enough to kill her. Lisa smiles through it all and leans in closer to Charles. Now that there's more at stake, Lisa needs to make sure her performance doesn't falter.

'I'll be here, Charles, waiting for you downstairs. Finally, we can be alone together without having to hide anything. Although I think Louise might suspect that something isn't right.'

'Don't worry about Louise,' he says smugly. 'I've got my cousin wrapped around my little finger.'

He hasn't, he just thinks he has. Louise rang Lisa a couple of weeks ago with concerns about Emma, knowing that Lisa is often at their house and spends so much time with Charles. Lisa was still surprised she went to her about it, though; she must have been desperate. Louise asked Lisa to keep an eye on things for her and promised that she would ruin Lisa's acting career if she told Charles about any of this. Louise had the contacts to do that. Lisa promised Louise she would do as she asked. She couldn't tell her that's what she was already doing anyway.

Lisa carefully pries the exact plan out of Charles so she can give her employer as much information as possible.

'The chef will prepare everything and place it on the trolley to go up to the bedroom,' he says. 'I'll choose the wine and pour two glasses ready before going in, and place them on the trolley in the correct positions. The trolley was a wedding gift; it has our names on either side, so there's no chance of getting the glasses mixed up. I'll mix the crushed pills in Emma's ready, and, voila,' he says, dramatically. 'Emma will be dead by dessert if all goes to plan.'

'God, Charles, you actually sound like you're enjoying this. Should I be worried?'

'Don't be silly, Lisa,' he says, wrapping his arms around her. Her skin crawls each time he touches her, but she never shows it.

'I have to leave early tonight,' she says. 'I should probably keep away until Wednesday now. We shouldn't draw any more attention to ourselves and risk ruining things now that we're so close.'

'I guess you might be right,' he admits. 'I'll miss you until then.'

'Of course you will,' she says with a smile.

*

The air outside feels so good in Lisa's lungs. She feels like she's just broken through the surface of an ocean she was drowning in. She wonders if Emma has any idea what Charles is planning. She's never struck Lisa as naive or gullible.

Lisa calls her employer as soon as she gets home, giving him all the new information she has. They discuss what to do next and how Lisa can try to save Emma. Lisa has struggled to steady her breathing since leaving Charles. Just a couple more days and this job will be over. She's so nervous now about how it will end. She had never expected it to go this far, but now she realises that either way, someone will die, and it's down to her who that will be. The plan now is to let Charles get everything ready, then distract him and switch the wine glasses.

* * *

*

Wednesday has come around too quickly. The nausea hasn't subsided since Emma found out that tonight is the night Charles is planning to kill her. She can't stop thinking about Marian and Charlie and how whatever the outcome is will affect their lives.

Molly's plan is to switch the drinks over tonight. Emma can tell that Molly is getting nervous as the time gets closer, even though she's reassured Emma she has absolutely no second thoughts or doubts about what she must do. What's making Molly so nervous is the thought of something going wrong and her letting Emma down. Emma feels awful for putting Molly in this position, but she could see no other way.

'I'll get you all dressed up tonight, Miss,' says Molly. 'Make you look all pretty, give you a bit of confidence to get through the evening. I'll get your red velvet gown out, shall I? The one with the gold trimmings on. You always look so beautiful in that. You'd be the belle of the ball if there was one.'

'That sounds lovely, Molly. Thank you.'

'I'll get your hair looking all nice too with your mother's gold brush.'

'I feel like I let my parents down with the way my life has turned out,' says Emma regretfully.

'Don't be silly, Miss. They loved you more than anything. They would be so proud of how strong you are. And you are, Miss. You always have been, deep down. Charles just made you forget that for a while.'

'Okay, Molly,' says Emma, lifting her chin a little higher. 'You're right, let's do this right tonight. Can you find my little purse and hair comb that match my dress, please? I want to look my best. Not for Charles, for me.'

'Of course, Miss. I'll get everything ready for you.' Molly takes Emma's hand and looks her in the eyes. 'I won't let you down tonight. You can count on me.'

Emma can't believe that it's come to this. Her life or Charles's. Her hands have been trembling all morning. She can't seem to relax at all, but she can't let Charles get suspicious that she knows anything. She has to remember her children and be strong for them. She focusses on that thought for the rest of the day.

*

Molly comes in to help Emma get ready, bringing a large glass of whisky for her to settle her nerves.

'Let's get you looking like a queen then, Miss.'

Molly helps Emma into her red gown, and offers her arm out to walk Emma over to the dressing table, where she brushes through her long waves, pinning some back and securing it with a red floral hair clip with shimmering golden leaves. Molly hands her her matching purse and ushers her to stand in front of the large mirror.

Emma's eyes fill up with tears. It's been so long since she's been able to get dressed up like this. She realises how much she's missed it.

'You look beautiful, Miss. Do you remember who you were now? Who you still are. I don't know how long those pills will take to kick in later, so you just carry on talking as normally as you can for as long as it takes. I won't be far away from the door all evening, so you call out if you need any help.'

'I'm ready, Molly,' she says assertively. All the anger about what Charles has done to her and plans to do to her burns away in her stomach. She no longer feels nervous, just furious and determined to take her life back.

*

* * *

Charles is pottering around in the kitchen, trying to look helpful, but mostly he's just making the staff uncomfortable with his presence. They clearly don't like being watched by him while they work. They keep shooting confused glances at each other and shrugging their shoulders.

Lisa hasn't long arrived. She heads straight for the kitchen, knowing that's where Charles will be. He greets her with a huge smile and leads her to a small table just outside the kitchen.

'Dinner's all ready,' he says eagerly. 'I'm just waiting for them to get the bottle of wine I asked for, then I'll be off to dine with Emma.'

When the trolley is ready to go, it's placed at the side of their table as Charles requested. He asks Lisa to get a glass so they can have a drink before he goes, but she knows why he really wants her to step away.

Just before Charles leaves, Lisa asks if he can pop into the next room to find her purse, which she left there on purpose. He always does as she asks, so he walks away with no suspicions. She quickly switches over his and Emma's wine glasses.

Molly is called to push the trolley up to the bedroom, accompanied by Charles. They enter Emma's room together, and Molly gives her a little nod, confirming her job is done before she leaves.

'Good evening, Miss. Enjoy your meal, both of you.'

Molly leaves, nervously glancing back at Emma as she closes the door after herself.

Now, Emma and Charles are alone.

'My...' he says, taking in Emma's appearance. 'You do still scrub up well, Emma. I'll give you that.'

'I think I'll take that as a compliment,' she says coolly.

'Well, we can chat later; there's plenty of time for that. We should get stuck into our food while it's still nice and hot.'

'Don't you want a drink first?' she asks curiously. She knows Charles will be impatient to get this over with. His eagerness to eat and the way he keeps looking at the plates, as though he's making sure they don't move on their own, makes her mind race. He's poisoned the food, not the wine.

'Of course,' he says, his eyes wandering around the room. He can't even look at her. 'A drink it is.' His eyes land on the photos of Emma's parents, and, for a moment, his mind appears to be elsewhere. Does he feel guilty? Charles always admired her father, who treated him well.

'What's wrong, Charles?' she asks.

'Do you still think about your parents much?'

'Of course I do, every day. Do you still think of my father? I know he meant a lot to you too.'

She wants to ask if he would be doing all of this if her father were still here, but she resists.

Charles gives his head a small shake and clears his throat, coming back to her and the situation in front of him.

'Are you ready to eat now?' he asks.

'After the wine,' she replies. 'Let's raise a toast first to the ones we've lost.'

They clink their glasses together, and Charles's attention is back on the food, but Emma tries to delay as calmly as she can.

'Another glass, Charles,' she says, 'before we eat. That one went down too quickly. It's been so long since I've tasted good wine.'

'Okay, just the one, Emma,' he says, frustration all over his face.

'Is my company really that bad that you can't wait to get away, Charles?'

'Don't be silly, Emma. We just don't really have much to talk about these days, do we?'

'And whose fault is that, Charles?'

'I don't want to argue tonight.'

'Neither do I.'

'Doesn't sound…like…it… I don't…'

'Charles, are you okay? You're looking a bit peaky, dear.'

'What have…you…done?' he says, trying to stand but stumbling into the trolley, his eyes wide with fear, a hand to his throat.

'Maybe it was the wine, or was it the food? Which one did you put the pills in, Charles? Can you remember?'

He looks straight into her eyes, confused and scared, his face turning a dark shade of red.

'How did…you…?'

'Know? It wasn't that hard to figure out, Charles. You faked this whole illness with that doctor friend of yours, poisoning my body with those pills you made me take every day. Did you really think that I wouldn't find out?'

'But…'

'But what? You put it in the food? Yes, I guessed that when you were so keen for me to eat immediately. You see, I've been hiding some of the pills for a while now, since you couldn't be bothered to watch me take them anymore. I kept them thinking they might come in handy one day. I didn't think I'd get the chance to give them back to you, but while you were dawdling, looking guiltily at the photo of my parents, I slipped them from my purse into your first glass of wine. Cheers, Charles,' she says, raising her glass to him. 'Here's to the end of your life, for plotting mine. I'm taking my life back and taking yours away.'

He's on the floor now, a terror on his face like nothing Emma has ever seen. Tears start to trail down her face. She doesn't even know what they're for. Sadness for her husband? Relief to get her life back finally? She sits and puts her head in her hands, letting it all out like a waterfall rushing to a stream, as her husband takes his final breath.

It seems like forever has passed when the doors burst open and Molly and Lisa rush in looking panicked, then relieved when they see Emma is okay. They both run over to her.

'Miss, what happened? We thought we had messed it up for you?'

Molly's whole body is shaking.

'We?' is all Emma manages to say. Her eyes dart from Molly to Lisa and back again.

'Lisa has been pretending to fall for Charles. It's a long story; she can tell you later. She said she switched your glasses over, but I had too. How did you know?'

'I didn't. He didn't put anything in the wine. It was in my food. He was so keen for me to eat it straight away, I just knew.'

Molly hugs Emma tightly, like she'll never let go.

'I'm so glad you're okay, Miss. I was so afraid when Lisa told me, we both were.'

'I don't understand,' Emma says, turning to Lisa.

'I wasn't in love with Charles,' says Lisa. 'It was a job; I'm an actress. Someone paid me to seduce your husband so I would have evidence for you and you could divorce him. They seemed to think that was what you wanted—a divorce. I had no idea that Charles would take it this far, but I got suspicious when you became ill, so I've been keeping an eye since.'

'Who paid you?' asks Emma.

'He said his name was John, but he didn't tell me his last name. I only ever spoke to him over the phone. Someone else delivers the money to me.'

Emma's head spins at the mention of John, the realisation of it all. She feels like she can't breathe.

'I switched the pills Charles had been giving you with sedatives,' Lisa says, 'harmless ones.'

'I don't know what to say.' Emma can't make sense of anything. 'Thank you, both of you.'

There's a moment of silence, and they all turn to the collapsed body in the corner.

'What do we do about him?' Emma asks quietly.

'Call the police and tell them mostly the truth,' says Molly quickly, like she's already thought it through. 'Tell them how he's been keeping you locked up, poisoning you, and trying to kill you. He just picked up the wrong glass.' Molly puts a kind hand on Emma's shoulder. 'It's all over now, Miss. This house can be your home again.'

*

Two months later

Telling the children was the hardest part for Emma. It was obviously quite a shock for them to learn what their father had done and that he was gone now, but mostly they were upset that they hadn't realised and helped their mother. She reassured them that they had kept her alive just by visiting her.

Charles was buried a week later. The funeral was surprisingly large, and Emma dutifully played the grieving widow. No one apart from those who were involved and her children know the truth about what happened, so Emma kept up appearances to avoid suspicion at the funeral. It wasn't the time or place.

She makes her way down the staircase she missed so much this morning and glances around the large hallway. She wants every room re-decorated with a fresh coat of paint to brighten it all back up a bit.

John will be arriving later. Everyone at the house calls him her saviour. He will be working in the gardens again, but not because she's paying him to. John will live here too, and the gardens will also belong to him.

John told Emma that Charles had tried to pay him to leave, then threatened to have him killed when he refused. He told Charles he changed his mind and took the money. John used the money to hire Lisa, who introduced herself to Louise before inserting herself into Charles and Emma's lives. Lisa was just meant to seduce Charles, get her proof, and then Emma could divorce him, but things changed drastically when Charles decided he wanted Emma dead. John had no choice but to let it play out. Nobody would believe him otherwise.

Emma's strength increases more and more every day now that she's able to step out into the daylight again. Every night when she gets ready for bed, she sits at her dressing table and brushes her hair, a hundred strokes a night. It reminds her of how strong she is now and how much strength it took to get here. Like the brush itself, she was made to last.

*

John joins her late when everyone else has retired for the night. They haven't told anyone about their relationship yet, but they plan to soon, when all the fuss over Charles has died down. She knows everyone will be happy for them, especially Molly.

Lisa still visits sometimes, updating Emma on her acting career. She's doing quite well now, though Emma's not surprised. She certainly had her fooled for a while. Lisa told Louise everything that happened, and neither of them have seen her since the funeral. Emma thinks she's too ashamed about what Charles did to her. She's assured her that she's more than welcome, but she can't seem to look Emma in the eye anymore.

Molly, her dearest Molly, has been fussing over her endlessly.

John gives Emma an engagement ring tonight, a beautiful ruby with diamonds around it that once belonged to his aunt.

Tomorrow they'll tell everyone the good news. The wedding will be a quiet one. She doesn't want a lavish occasion like she had with Charles. Just herself, John, the kids, and the people closest to her. They'll have the ceremony in their garden.

*

Now when Emma gets out of bed in the morning, it feels like a different house to the one she was held prisoner in for so long. Everything is bright again, the sun rushing around every inch of the bedroom when she opens the curtains, highlighting every sparkle and every detail in the room. Once again, her dressing table looks covered in treasures, the light bringing everything to life again.

Emma and John sit together in the garden with their tea, waiting for Marian and Charlie to arrive so they can tell them their good news.

'I think we should spend their visit out here today,' says Emma. 'It's such a nice day. It would be a shame to waste it. Marian loves spending time out here too. I guess I forgot that for a while, not being able to come out here myself. I forgot a lot of things.'

'Well, it's over now, Emma,' John says, placing his hand on hers. 'He can't hurt you anymore.'

'I know,' she says. 'It was just an awful time, and I can't believe how happy I am now. I worry that something will ruin it.'

'That'll never happen. I know I can't promise nothing bad will ever happen again, but I can promise that I would never hurt you, not like Charles did.'

She holds her hand against his cheek and closes her eyes.

'I know you won't,' she says.

She's startled by the sound of distant footsteps and voices approaching them. Marian and Charlie smile and wave as they walk along the path towards them. All of Emma's doubts disappear.

*

It's a beautiful day for a wedding. Emma wears a simple, white, long satin dress and a headband decorated with white roses. Charlie walks Emma down the aisle, between the rows of chairs laid out in the garden, with Marian and Molly following behind them. Emma has hired extra help for the day, so that her regular staff can attend the ceremony and afterparty as her friends. They've always been more of a family to her than Charles ever was.

All of their guests watch as Emma and John stand before them, reading their vows. All Emma can see is stars. Maybe it's just the sun shining in her eyes making everything sparkle, but to Emma, they're stars. Molly sobs through the entire ceremony, and even the chef sheds a little tear, though he tries to hide it.

They eat out in the garden around large tables after the ceremony. A band plays music, and everyone dances and drinks the rest of the day away. By 9pm, Charlie wanders off upstairs to sleep, too intoxicated to drive home. Marian leaves shortly after with everyone else, after telling Emma and John what a wonderful time she's had and how happy she is for them. Emma knows Marian loved her father, even if the feelings became complicated after finding out what he'd done, so her words mean a lot to Emma.

It's finally time for Emma and John to retreat to their bed, all the guests gone, and the new staff cleaning up the garden ready for the morning. They both have a giggle about being too tired for any marital bliss on their wedding night. Despite traditions, they are no strangers to each other in the bedroom, so tonight is just another night, where they decide it's perfectly fine to nod off to sleep in each other's arms. The day has been special enough. They're happy to end the day this way.

'Goodnight, Mrs Garcia,' says John, eyes already closed, somewhere between asleep and awake.

'Goodnight, Mr Garcia,' Emma replies, sinking into her new husband's arms, joining him in a peaceful sleep, knowing she is safe and loved.

*

They continue to act like a pair of teenagers in love after their wedding, rarely spending any time apart. Emma has a small summer house built where the old tennis court once stood next to the garden, which becomes a place for her to read peacefully.

Marian and Charlie visit a lot more now since Charles has gone. Emma loves spending so much time with them. She wonders if, after everything, they feel they need to check in on her more often and make sure she's safe and well. They're always concerned about her health, even though she feels better than she ever has.

The end of summer is approaching, but the heat still lingers on, forcing Emma to head back to the house earlier than usual today. The heat was making her feel sleepy, so she goes up to her old bedroom. She hasn't been in here since she was forced to stay in it for all those months, but it's out of the sunlight and offers a cooler temperature than the bedroom she shares with John.

She sits down on the bed, removing her shoes, and that old painting Charles bought for her catches her eye. It always gave her a strange feeling that she could never quite explain, like it was watching her.

She pulls her eyes away and tells herself she's being ridiculous. It's just a painting. It only takes her a few minutes to drift off to sleep. She falls into a horrible dream that someone's trying to choke her, but is it a dream? She jolts awake suddenly, opening her eyes to see smoke coming in around the door. She rushes off the bed, opens the door, and finds herself, once again, trapped in her bedroom. The door won't open, no matter what she tries. John is working in the garden, and the staff are all down in the kitchen. Nobody can hear her scream for help.

Is this Charles's final revenge? She'd forgotten all about the painting until now, but now she feels like her eyes are being drawn to it, just like before she fell asleep. Then she remembers: You will lose someone you love. Charles and Emma had no love for each other by the end. When he died, she had assumed that was it and the curse had lived up to its threat, but Emma loves John, and John loves her.

Her final thoughts before she is overcome by the smoke are of John and her children and how she wishes she had gotten rid of that painting before it was too late.

*

A few weeks later, John finds the courage to re-enter the bedroom where Emma had been trapped for so long and where she had died. The painting immediately catches his eye. He remembers Emma telling him of some silly curse they had both shrugged off as nonsense. He asks the cleaning staff to take it away, so the painting is removed, unscathed from the fire that damaged most of the upstairs of their house.

Charlie takes ownership of the home with John's blessing, but John continues to live there and work in the garden, keeping it beautiful, like he knows Emma would have wanted.

Clara

Emma and Charles's story turned out to be quite a drama, but Clara enjoyed it. She enjoyed the powerful feeling of being able to manipulate them all without them even knowing she was there. Most people seemed to get some kind of reaction from looking at the painting; some felt unsure, some were fascinated, but they didn't know why. Some people just got spooked by it. Maybe they were the ones that got to see a glimpse of her thoughts for a second.

Charles was Clara's first choice to die. The man was evil and didn't deserve to be loved by anyone after what he did to his wife. However, seeing how relieved Emma was when he was finally gone, Clara wasn't satisfied that enough damage had been done. If anything, Emma had been rescued and could go on to live a happy life with John. But why should Emma get to move on? Clara had to live the rest of her days buried beneath the memories of her husband's betrayal. It didn't seem fair that Emma would just bounce back and move on just like that. Clara was very dissatisfied with this outcome. She needed someone else to suffer—really suffer; otherwise, it wouldn't have felt like the curse had truly taken effect.

Emma was the next obvious choice. John loved her, really loved her, and she loved him. Someone's heart had to shatter the way Clara's had. That's the whole point of this, she thought; it had to hurt. She did like Emma, even though she tried not to. She was stronger than Clara had ever been, and Clara almost wanted her to succeed at recovering fully from everything Charles did to her, but seeing her happy with John only rekindled the fire in Clara's belly and the desire to see everyone suffer.

That was her first time playing out the curse on someone, and it was all a learning process for her. She found out how much influence she could really have over a person and how to use it. There have been many times over the years now, but that was one that stuck in Clara's mind. The significant ones stayed with her through time. Some lives just seemed to get to her more than others. She didn't know why. Maybe it was the way they lived or acted, or maybe she was able to see deeper into their souls than the others. She envied Emma and her strength a little. Clara always believed she was a strong woman when she was very young. She grew up with her own stubborn ideas of what her life would be. She always wanted to live on a farm and work on it together with a husband who she loved and loved her back. She wanted to raise chickens and other animals. Tend to them, collect eggs in the mornings, and really get stuck into the work. That surprised some people; they thought she would be afraid to get her hands dirty, but she never had the desire to walk around in fancy gowns, wasting her days away while paying other people to do all her work for her. Yes, her family had the wealth for her to live that kind of life, but it was never what she wanted. She found it all quite dull.

That's how Jack was different from the rest of the men she had met before him. Her parents didn't approve at first, but Jack won them over eventually with his charm and his seemingly unwavering love for their daughter. They set them up on a large farm that had everything she wanted and allowed her to live the life she had dreamed of.

Jack said he admired Clara's willingness to work when she didn't have to. She doubted that later on. He started to change her bit by bit. It was subtle at first; she didn't even notice herself changing. He would do it by spoiling her and flattering her. He'd encourage her to take days off, offering to take her shopping instead, buying her beautiful dresses and expensive jewellery, until one day she barely recognised herself. She was becoming everything she didn't want to be: a proper lady. He had hired men to help on the farm and tried to encourage her to do less. That's when he started convincing her to go to town more too, for shopping trips or dinner with friends. She later wondered how she hadn't seen what he was doing. The signs were all there, the cracks small and barely noticeable at first. Maybe Clara didn't see it because she didn't want to. She realised later that it was obvious he was just trying to get rid of her during the day.

When Clara left, she kept in touch with her parents and went into hiding, although Jack never tried to find her anyway. They forced Jack out of the farm. He had no power to fight against them; they had paid for it all in the first place, so it had never really belonged to him. Her parents sold it, which broke Clara's heart all over again, though she knew she would never be able to return. Instead, they bought her a little house in a quiet village, far enough away that she never had to hear about Jack and his new wife, but close enough that her parents were able to visit regularly. The house was remote and quiet and peaceful; no one bothered her there. Clara bought a few chickens to keep in her garden. She tried, at first, to make the best of the situation. She tried to make her own little peaceful life away from the bad memories, but word got round of how she came to be there, as it always does, and the locals began to look at her differently, like they felt sorry for her. She started avoiding them more and more, trying to avoid their sympathetic glances, but the more isolated she became, the more time she had to think about just how much Jack had ruined her life and how miserable she had become. The need for revenge spiralled out of control more and more as time went on.

When she awoke one day in Emma's beautiful home, she knew the curse had worked. She didn't know who the people in this house were yet, and she didn't care. She couldn't wait to get to work and make them all suffer. She became enthralled with spending her time watching these people who had no idea she was even there, seeing how they reacted to the painting on close inspection. She wondered if they could feel her presence at all or see her staring back at them. She learnt quickly that she could make them feel however she wanted them to feel. If she wanted someone to feel insecure or afraid, she could do that. She could make someone feel enchanted by the painting, making it hard for them to look away from her. The power made her feel more alive than when she was actually alive.

A couple of homes later, she ended up in the middle of another troubled relationship, the marriage of Eva and Rob. At this point, Clara had already had a few experiences and a few owners and had gotten into the swing of it all. She was enjoying every minute and eager to get to the next home. They weren't quite as interesting as Emma and Charles, but she couldn't choose where she ended up, so she had to try to make the most of it. Eva had a sharp tongue that Clara couldn't help but be impressed by sometimes, but she wasn't there to be impressed. She was there to cause tragedy and devastation, and it was time to get to work.

Eva & Robert

Eva peers across the restaurant, visibly disappointed with the other people here. Her husband, Robert, sits across from her, tapping his fingers on the table, waiting for her to say she wants to leave. Robert doesn't see the appeal of these overpriced restaurants with their tiny portions, but he tags along to keep Eva happy. Eva orders the dishes with the fewest calories, always keeping an eye on her figure. Robert tries to make the most of the menu. He's sure Eva hates watching him eat as much as he likes, but he may as well enjoy it if he has to be here.

He ponders the decline of their relationship as he watches her hopefully looking around, waiting for someone important to walk in, paying no attention to him at all. He wonders if the kind and fun-loving woman he fell in love with is still in there somewhere, before her acting career started to take off and it became all she cared about. If the old Eva is still in there, she doesn't show her often. Lately, he's just someone to accompany her around town so that she doesn't have to appear in public alone.

'Are you ready to leave?' he asks, his empty dessert bowl in front of him. Eva didn't have dessert.

'I guess we could go,' she replies, still not looking at him. 'There doesn't seem to be anything happening here tonight. I don't see any familiar faces. I thought this was supposed to be the place to be at the moment.'

Eva thinks she's more famous than she actually is, with only a few small roles under her belt and no lead parts in the pipeline, though not for lack of trying.

'We can stay for another drink if you'd like, see if anyone turns up.' Robert always makes an effort still, even now when he knows there's no point.

'No, I think I'd rather just have a glass of wine back at

home maybe,' she says reluctantly, her eyes still darting around the restaurant, hoping to see someone she hadn't spotted before, someone who could help boost her career.

Eva puts so much effort into her appearance for their outings, so Robert can see why she would be disappointed when, in her mind, it's all for nothing. It's not like no one notices her, just not anyone Eva would deem important. She doesn't notice anymore all of the admiring glances from other people around her, people she would say are less important, but they obviously have big money or they wouldn't get through the door of a place like this. They're just not in the right business.

Tonight, she's wearing a strapless, sapphire, chiffon dress that clings to her body perfectly. Below the belt, the material flows out into a full, knee-length skirt. She dresses it up with a sparkling diamond necklace that fits close around her neckline and matches her diamond stud earrings. Her curled, black hair sits neatly above her shoulders, not a strand out of place. She finishes off her glamorous look with bold red lipstick, which suits her so well. She truly is a vision. Many pass by and give a quick glance before doing a double take, trying to take all of her in.

Robert and Eva have been married for five years now, but, for Robert, it feels like longer. It was the classic love story; they met at a young age and were both head over heels. Robert was besotted with her. They went to dances, spent long summer days at the beach, and wanted to spend every waking moment together. Robert is a photographer and was always taking her picture back then. Their relationship took a hit when Eva got her first acting job. Robert was genuinely excited for her at first, but then her career became all she thought about. It had nothing to do with the money; she had plenty of that from her parents. She just loved the attention and glamour that came with it. She told Robert that she wanted to be a star and that it would come before anything else. This meant children were out of the question. Robert wanted them, but what Robert wanted didn't matter anymore.

That's when he realised that this marriage wasn't going to last forever. He wants a family and grandchildren someday. He can't have that if his wife doesn't want it.

Grace isn't like Eva. Robert met Grace at a jewellery store a few weeks ago while he was shopping for a gift for Eva's birthday. Robert was immediately struck with Grace when he entered the store and saw her standing behind the counter. He thought it was love at first sight. He knew from the first glance that he would never be able to forget an inch of her porcelain face and rosy, pink lips. Her golden blonde hair curled to just below her shoulders, and her emerald, green eyes made you feel like you could see into her soul. Or that's how they made Robert feel anyway. He could barely speak when Grace asked if she could help him, the words getting lost on the way to his mouth. When he finally caught his breath back, it felt like a new part of his life had just begun, right there in that moment.

He realised he must have been staring because Grace's cheeks turned a deep shade of pink. He didn't want to tell Grace he was there to buy a present for his wife, so he lied and said he was looking for a gift for his mother instead. His mother wouldn't even approve of him being in such an expensive jewellery store.

'A string of plastic beads can make a woman shine as much as diamonds if she's beautiful on the inside,' she would always tell him.

He ended up saying he wasn't sure what kind of thing he was looking for after getting more flustered when Grace started asking questions. He said maybe he'd go for a coffee to think about it. Then he surprised them both by asking if she would like to join him, and Grace surprised them both by saying yes. He was taken aback when she immediately removed her apron and hung it up.

'Mr Crawford?' she called to someone out the back of the store. 'I'm taking my break now, if that's okay?'

After the initial uncomfortable shyness in the store, they suddenly felt at ease when they stepped outside, like they were old friends going for a coffee to catch up after some time apart.

As they sat with their coffees in the diner around the corner, Robert admitted that he hadn't been completely honest with her and that he was really looking for a gift for his wife. He told her how they'd grown apart and that this would probably be the last gift he would buy for her before they go their separate ways. Grace said that if the marriage ended, he could call into the store again and arrange to meet up for another coffee someday.

'It already is over,' he told her.

They agreed to meet for coffee once a week until things were finalised with him and Eva.

'There's no harm in just meeting up as friends, right?' he said.

'No, I guess not,' she replied, in a voice so soft he thought he could close his eyes and listen to her talking forever.

Robert didn't go back to the jewellery store after the diner. He went to a small antique store on the way home instead and bought a painting he thought Eva might like. He wasn't sure what made him think she would like it. It showed a family playing together at the beach, but there was something about it that he couldn't put his finger on. His eyes kept going back to it as he walked around the store, and he stood in front of it for a while, admiring all the eye-catching details. He couldn't tear his eyes away; he felt like he had to buy it.

The days Robert doesn't spend with Grace have begun to

feel like stepping stones leading to his new favourite day of the week, the day he has coffee with her in his new favourite diner.

He soaks up every moment of their time together. He can't believe how lucky he is to have met her, how he happened to walk into the jewellery store she worked in, and how she agreed to have coffee with him.

Robert realises his mind has been wandering, but Eva hasn't really noticed.

'Actually, maybe we could stay for one more drink, if you don't mind,' she says, snapping him back to the present.

'Sure, one for the road, then home to a bottle of wine, yes?'

'Okay,' she agrees.

She's clearly still hoping for someone to turn up and notice her, probably thinking what a waste of time and effort it was getting all glammed up for nothing, again.

*

Eva's been watching Robert closely for a couple of weeks now. Well, not her personally, but the PI she's hired. Robert thinks she doesn't know him, that she doesn't pay attention to him, but she couldn't not notice that he's been in his own little dream world lately, and she knew it wasn't because of her.

The PI brought her photographs of Robert and Grace at a diner; they seem to meet at the same time in the same place every week. Going by the photos, the girl is pretty, but in a very normal kind of way—nothing special or glamorous about her. Maybe that's what he wants, Eva thinks, a boring housewife in the making, but she refuses to be made a fool of. She can just imagine the headlines now: Movie Star's Husband Caught Cheating With Jewellery Store Assistant. She doesn't want the pity; she doesn't need it.

Eva doesn't know how serious Robert is about Grace yet. They look very cosy in the photos, but they only ever seem to meet in public. The way he's been walking around entranced with that silly grin on his face, though, Eva has to assume he's fallen quickly.

As she mulls over how she feels about all of this and what she should do about it, she decides a bit of retail therapy might lift her spirits, maybe some new jewellery. She knows just the store she wants to visit.

When she enters, there are no employees on the shop floor, but she can hear voices coming from the back. She casually walks around, inspecting the contents of each glass case. She was hoping it would be one of those stores that's full of cheap trash—a reflection of some of the employees, maybe. Instead, she's dazzled by the sparkling diamonds and gemstones before her, twinkling like the fullest sky of stars you could ever see. Now she actually envies Grace for getting to work in such a beautiful place. Not that Grace could afford any of this on her salary, she's sure.

It saddens her for a moment that Robert probably came here initially to buy a birthday present for Eva, and, instead, got distracted by a pretty blonde behind the counter. He ended up getting her a painting, which she does love. It's not something she would usually appreciate, but she can't help gazing at it for a while every day. Something about it steadies her breathing in the morning and prepares her for the day. She doesn't understand why, but that's how it feels.

'Can I help?' a soft voice asks from across the store.

'No, thank you. I'm just looking,' replies Eva, as she turns around to see Grace standing behind the counter, smiling politely at her as Eva looks her up and down. 'Actually, I'm looking for something nice to wear to a party next week. It'll be a very elegant occasion, so it has to be something special.'

'Of course, I'm sure we can find something special and

elegant for you, Madam,' says Grace in her sickeningly sweet voice.

'Madam makes me sound like a grandmother. Call me Eva.'

You can almost hear the penny drop as Grace realises who's standing in front of her. Eva watches as Grace tries to avoid making eye contact with her, her cheeks reddening, and her hands clasped tightly in front of her.

'Of course,' says Grace. 'Sorry, Eva.'

'Well, what would you suggest then? You do have some lovely pieces here.'

'Thank you,' replies Grace.

'Well, that's not really a compliment to you, is it dear? You just work here.'

'No, sorry, I mean…'

'Stop babbling,' interrupts Eva. 'I haven't got all day. Can you show me some pieces before I completely lose interest?'

'Yes, of course. If you come this way,' says Grace, almost stumbling over her own feet. Eva smirks to herself, thinking how easily rattled Grace is. Robert must like the timid, clumsy type then.

Grace pulls out a tray of pure sparkle from behind the counter. Eva is so in awe of the display in front of her that she almost forgets why she came here in the first place.

'As you can see, we have some beautiful pieces here. I'm sure each one would look lovely on you.'

'I'm sure they would. They are lovely. Maybe I'll come back with my husband. I'm sure he wouldn't mind buying something special for me. He's always so generous,' says Eva, looking directly into Grace's eyes.

Grace shifts from one foot to the other and clears her throat.

'Well, you're very lucky. So you won't be purchasing anything today?

Eva looks back at the case of beautiful jewellery Grace has presented her with.

'Tempting as it is, not today. Sorry if that loses you commission or points with your boss.'

'Not at all. We don't work on commission here.'

'Maybe one day you'll find someone who will buy you jewellery like this. What do you think?'

'I'm not really bothered about wearing expensive jewellery, to be honest.'

'Of course you're not,' says Eva sarcastically, looking her up and down again. 'Some women are happy to wear cheap costume jewellery, I guess.'

'You can get some that look just as pretty as anything we have in here,' replies Grace timidly.

'Nothing sparkles like a diamond. Anyway, I won't be buying anything today. Maybe I'll come another time when someone who actually knows and appreciates the value of jewellery is working here.'

Grace looks deflated, like she wants to say something but thinks better of it. Job done. Eva leaves feeling pleased with herself. She decides to treat herself to a cup of coffee and a slice of cake in a diner just around the corner from the jewellery store, realising when she steps inside that this must be where Robert meets Grace.

As she sits with her coffee, she contemplates her options going forward. She can't let Robert divorce her. There would be too much bad publicity; it would make her look weak and pathetic. She knows she's not that well established in the movie business yet, and this isn't how she wants to gain more attention. She can't be portrayed as the poor, betrayed wife.

Eva decides she just needs to get rid of Grace. She's like a weak little kitten anyway, so it shouldn't be too hard to scare her away. Maybe Eva will visit her again soon and make her believe that Robert has decided to stay with her. She seems gullible enough to believe anything anyone tells her.

*

When Robert gets to the diner today, Grace is quiet and fidgety and can't seem to look him in the eye. She tells him about her run-in with Eva.

'She was awful. She must know about us.'

'Eva is horrible to everyone,' says Robert unconcerned. 'Trust me, it's just the way she is. And a jewellery store like yours is exactly her kind of thing. I don't think it's connected at all, probably just a coincidence.'

Grace doesn't look a bit convinced. He watches her eyes glisten as they fill with tears she desperately tries to hold back.

'Grace, please don't let her get to you. If she does know, then this is exactly what she wants. I can't confront her until I know for sure that she does know something, but I don't think she would be able to keep quiet about it. She would probably enjoy tearing me apart if she knew about us.'

'I'm sorry, Robert,' says Grace, her voice quavering, 'but until I know for sure, we need to take a break from meeting for a while. I just can't do this. I don't want to be blamed for breaking up a marriage.'

'You're not, Grace,' says Robert, leaning forward with desperation in his eyes. 'It's already over, I told you that. Even if I hadn't met you, I would still want a divorce.'

Grace doesn't reply. She just takes hold of Rob's hand, and they sit there quietly for a while.

'Please come and see me next week,' he says. 'Even if it's just to find out what's going on. Please?'

'I don't know,' she says quietly.

'Believe me, I know Eva can be intimidating, I'm just used to it. I forget how she can come across to people who don't know her.'

'I can't do that again. She can't keep coming in the shop like that. She might get me fired. I'll spend every day watching that door now, afraid it'll be her coming back for round two.'

'She won't,' he says. 'I'll tell her tonight that I want a divorce and confront her about her visit. I can't put it off forever, and I don't want her upsetting you again.'

'Are you sure that's a good idea right now?'

'I'm sure, Grace,' he says, brushing a loose strand of hair away from her face. 'I've been wanting to do it for so long. It'll be a relief to not have to pretend anymore.'

*

When Robert gets home, Eva is reading on a sun lounger in the garden wearing a bikini and a light floral kimono. Her sunglasses cover her eyes, so Robert can't read her expression.

'I hear you went jewellery shopping today,' he says. 'Did you find what you were looking for?'

She puts her book down.

'Subtle Robert,' she sneers. 'And who did you hear that from, I wonder? Wouldn't happen to be a cute little store assistant named Grace, would it? Did she run crying to you after your mean wife was so nasty to her?' Eva pulls a mock sad face and chuckles. 'I thought I was quite reserved, to be honest, considering she's screwing my husband.'

Eva gets up and walks into their living room with Robert following behind her. She makes herself comfortable on the sofa, and he sits on the chair opposite.

'She's not screwing anyone. We just meet up for coffee once a week, that's it.' Robert sighs and softens his voice. 'We both know that our marriage hasn't been good for a while now.

Neither of us wants to be in this marriage anymore.'

'But we are in this marriage,' replies Eva, 'and you are not going to embarrass me by making headlines with your mistress.'

'Then just give me a divorce, and what I do will no longer reflect on you.'

'It'll still get about, people will still talk.'

Robert stands up, pacing in front of her and shaking his head.

'I'm sorry, Eva, but you've forced me to say this. You're really not that famous. I don't think anyone would care enough to write about your marriage, let alone for it to make headlines.'

She coolly removes her sunglasses, and Robert swears he can see red around her pupils for a second. What the hell was he thinking speaking to her like that?

'I am more important than you think. You just don't understand how it all works. You're oblivious to everything that goes on around you. I won't be giving you a divorce yet, and if you continue to see that pathetic excuse of a woman, you'll never get one. A divorce will be on my terms when I decide the time is right. Maybe when I meet someone else. That would be a different kind of scandal, wouldn't it? Especially if it was another movie star.'

She's no longer looking at Robert. Her eyes have glazed over as she imagines all the different scenarios of how this could play out. Robert's losing patience with her and the whole situation.

'Can't you just pretend to be with someone else? Just a publicity stunt to take the attention away from me and put it on you?'

She glares at him again, the corner of her mouth slipping into a smirk. 'We really are desperate to get away, aren't we?'

'Please, Eva.'

'Don't beg Robert. It's not very becoming.'

Robert sits back down, defeated, with his head in his hands. He's run out of words to try to convince her to give him what he wants, and she's enjoying every minute of it.

'I could just leave, you know,' he says finally. 'Even if you don't agree to a divorce, I could just pack a bag and stay at a hotel for a while, until I find something permanent. You can't make me stay here.'

'If you do that, I will make Grace's life hell. You know I will.'

Robert knows he can't react and knows it's pointless arguing with her anymore or trying to reason with her. His fists clench at his side, his fingernails digging into the palms of his hands. His whole body is tense. She stands up and turns towards the painting he bought her for her birthday. He unclenches his fists and watches her for a moment, trying to calm himself.

'I know you were disappointed I didn't get you jewellery or something more personal,' he says.

'You're wrong. I love the painting actually, and it does feel personal to me. I have no idea why, but it does. It feels like the most important gift you've ever given me. Does that sound weird?' she asks.

'I don't think so. I find myself looking at it more often than I thought I would.'

There's a silence as Eva continues to gaze at the painting and Robert watches her.

'I did love you once, you know,' he says.

'I know you did,' replies Eva. 'I loved you too. I think I probably still do a little, but it's not the same anymore.'

'I would like to see you happy, Eva, even if it is with someone else.'

Eva turns to face Robert, and he's surprised to see her face has softened and her eyes are slightly red.

'Okay,' she says decidedly. 'Give me a few weeks to decide how best to handle all this and... I will give you a divorce. But we do it my way, and you have to be patient.'

Robert tries not to look too happy about this. He doesn't want to do or say anything that will make her change her mind.

'Thank you, Eva. Can I just ask, why the wait?'

'Because I need to clear my head and make sure the plan is efficient and believable. I'll drop word around that we've not been getting along lately. That way, we can make it look amicable, not like you're leaving me for another woman.'

'Okay,' says Robert, nodding. 'A few weeks. If you go back on it then, though, I will just leave.'

'Fine. You'll still accompany me out some evenings for now, though, right? And you can't see Grace until then.'

'Okay, but I will have to let her know what's going on next week.'

He sees her face hardening once again, but she doesn't crack.

'Fine.'

Robert is wary that Eva might change her mind, but he tries to focus on the positive. If all goes to plan, after a few weeks he will finally be able to leave, and he can spend more time with Grace then.

'I'm going out with Isabelle tonight,' says Eva, checking the time on her watch. 'In fact, I'd better get ready.' Isabelle never comes here to get ready for their nights out anymore. The last time she was here, she was acting a bit strange, telling Eva to get rid of the painting Robert had bought for her. She said it had an evil aura about it, which Eva couldn't help but laugh at. Isabelle was never spooked by anything. Eva put it down to jealousy, maybe, of her marriage with Robert. Even though Isabelle knew it had become a sham, she also knew that it had started from a place of love all those years ago.

She leaves Robert contemplating his thoughts and what will happen next. Overall, that conversation went better than he had expected it to. He'd half-expected to have to physically defend himself after threatening to leave, but Eva took it quite well. The tension in Robert's shoulders eases; the end is in sight.

*

Eva's tongue sticks to the roof of her mouth, and her eyes itch with the remains of last night's make up. Her head aches with its own weight as she tries to lift it, scanning the room with half-open eyes. She doesn't remember how she got home from her night out with Isabelle. A lot of their nights out together end that way. Isabelle can be such a bad influence, but she's so much more fun to be around than Robert. In some ways, Eva would love to tell Robert about her and Isabelle, how their long-term friendship had blossomed into more than that when they both revealed their romantic feelings for each other a couple of months ago. At the same time, she wouldn't trust him to not tell anyone, and she can't let that get around. It's probably the real reason she couldn't make her marriage with Robert work in the end. Eva could see Isabelle all the time if she was divorced, and nobody would know; just two party girls out for dinner. The thought of the scandal that would occur if it ever got out sends shivers down her spine, but neither of them are stupid about it. They know how to behave in public to avoid suspicion.

Robert thinks he's going to get everything he wants, but he's not. Eva's going to have some fun with Grace again today. She's going to make sure that Grace leaves Robert and stays away from him for good.

* * *

*

Eva can't pretend she doesn't enjoy the expression on Grace's face when she enters the store again, the smile on her face shattering like a glass ornament. Eva almost feels sorry for her, but not quite.

'Hi Grace, you remember me, right? Don't worry, I won't take up too much of your time,' says Eva, making her way towards the counter, Grace frozen where she stands. 'I've just come with a message from Robert. You know Robert, right? My husband? Of course you do. He said he won't be seeing you again. You see, he loves me, and we've just been going through a bad patch recently. Oh, don't look so upset, dear, you're not the first and probably won't be the last woman he's enjoyed a brief flirtation with, but he always comes back to me. I'm sorry you got taken in by him. I know he can be very convincing. He plays the part so well, doesn't he? The lonely husband with the mean wife.'

'I'm sorry, I thought you…'

'You thought what, dear? That we were separating? No offence, but look at me and look at you. Why would he trade down? He was just slumming it with you for a while, a brief excitement. I know that sounds harsh, but you're making a fool of yourself, and you need to stick to guys more suited to you, if you know what I mean.'

Grace's shoulders slump and her head hangs low. All she can manage to reply is a quiet, 'I'm sorry'.

'Stop saying sorry, it's annoying. Here,' says Eva, handing Grace a handkerchief, 'clean yourself up. Look, just forget about Robert and get on with your life. I'll say no more about this if you just do that. You won't have to see either of us again.'

'Okay,' says Grace, her voice barely above a whisper. Her face has turned a pale white, and Eva half-expects her to collapse to the floor. Grace's boss walks in from the back of the store and gives Grace a concerned glance.

'I don't think your assistant is feeling very well,' says Eva to the boss. 'Maybe you could get her a chair to sit down on for a minute.'

'Grace, are you okay?'

'I'm fine, just a little dizzy,' says Grace, avoiding eye contact with the boss and with Eva.

'I'm going to leave you to take care of her. I need to get home to my husband,' says Eva, glaring at Grace as she throws her a quick look of understanding. 'Goodbye, Grace.'

Eva's surprised at how much she enjoyed breaking that poor girls heart on Robert's behalf, and he doesn't even know about it.

She decides to treat herself to a glass of wine back at home, despite it still being morning. Robert isn't around, so he must be working in the studio today. She contemplates the idea of keeping Robert around longer than she had agreed to. She likes that she has a cover story to hide her relationship with Isabelle. It makes her feel safer. She does actually quite like having Robert's company around the house sometimes. Despite this indiscretion with Grace, he has been a good husband, and she considers him a good friend to have. If she could be nicer to him, maybe he'll feel the same about her too. She doesn't even know why she's so cold towards him; he's really not a bad guy.

As Eva looks out into the garden that evening, she realises Grace will have to go for the sake of her reputation. She calls Isabelle straight away to tell her about her decision. Eva notes the tinge of sadness in Isabelle's voice, but she said she understands.

Eva wonders if her visit to Grace earlier will be enough to keep her away or if she will have to go back. She's hoping Grace will find a different job and disappear, somewhere

Robert won't be able to find her. Eva hears the door opening and closing as Robert returns home from work. She greets him with a smile at the door, causing confusion and suspicion to spread across his face.

She offers him a drink, which he accepts, and they sit together at the kitchen table.

'I just want to say,' says Eva, 'that for the next few weeks, I would love it if we could just get along. Maybe become friends again. What do you think?'

Robert frowns at her and takes a sip of his whisky.

'Seems a bit late for that now, don't you think?'

'I know, but I really don't want us to part on bad terms. We have a history, and we know each other.'

'I'm not sure I do know you all that well anymore,' says Robert honestly. 'I think I lost the real you somewhere along the way. You started hiding yourself from me. You turned into someone else.'

Eva feels surprisingly stung by his words.

'I know, and I'm sorry. I do regret the way I've behaved towards you. Can we put it all behind us?'

'If you really mean it, we can see how it goes. I've never wanted to fight with you.'

'So, friends?'

'Friends,' he nods, but he's still looking at Eva like she's up to something. Eva realises she's really going to have to put the effort in for this new plan to work. Eva can be there for him while he gets over the loss of Grace. That might bring them closer if he can find some comfort in Eva.

*

'Still here then?' Grace looks just as mortified as usual to see Eva standing in the doorway.

'Where else would I be?' says Grace, with a bold new

attitude Eva hasn't seen from her before. There's still a timidity to her voice and body language though that stops Eva taking her too seriously, like a child testing boundaries and seeing how much they can push back. 'Don't worry, I haven't seen Robert.'

'Is that attitude I hear in your little voice, Grace?'

'You can say what you like. I don't care anymore. Why are you even here anyway? To check that Robert isn't still coming to see me? I don't want anything to do with him anymore. You made it pretty clear where I stand last time.'

'I'm just checking that you got the message. You seem like the clingy type. Look, why don't you go make a fresh start for yourself somewhere? Forget about Robert and what he's done to you. There must be somewhere you'd rather be than here? I could help you financially if you need it.'

'Why would you do that?'

'Look, I know it's not your fault. Robert can be pretty charming when he wants to be. Wouldn't you find it easier to forget about him if you were somewhere else? Somewhere neither of us could turn up at any moment?'

'I don't know,' says Grace, looking from Eva to the store and back again. 'I like my job and my boss. I don't really want to leave, and I've not done anything wrong, so I shouldn't have to.'

'Well, think about it, and I mean, really think about it,' says Eva, with a cold, threatening smile. 'I'll come by tomorrow afternoon to see if you've made a decision.

She doesn't give Grace a chance to answer. She just heads out the door and doesn't look back.

*

Robert has missed Grace so much this last week. He's on his way to the diner where he's supposed to meet her today, but he's had a bad feeling all morning that she won't be there. He decides to meet her at the store instead, so they can walk over together if she still wants to see him.

He can tell by the look on her face that something's wrong as soon as he walks in. Her smile and sparkle in her eyes are not there. She looks pale and nervous when she sees him. He can see her shoulders tense and her body stiffen.

'What's wrong, Grace? I thought I'd meet you here today, so we could walk to the diner together.'

'I'm not going anywhere with you, Robert,' she says as firmly as she can, a slight tremor in her voice. 'I know you don't love me and that you've done this to your wife before with other women.'

Robert can't quite believe what he's hearing.

'What? What are you…'

'Eva told me all about your flings.'

The whole thing is so ridiculous that Robert would laugh if it didn't appear that Grace had been sucked in by Eva and actually believed whatever crazy story she had told her.

'Grace, come on, you know I'm not like that. I love you,' says Robert so earnestly that Grace is almost brought back to reality, but she's clearly torn and can't decide who to believe anymore. 'Please don't believe her lies. I told you how devious she can be, didn't I?'

Robert tries to take Grace's hand in his but she slowly withdraws it.

'She told me you made all that stuff up.'

'And you believe that after her coming here and talking to you the way she did?' Robert realises his voice is getting louder the more frustrated he's getting. An elderly lady who's browsing in the store looks over at him with a raised eyebrow. He guides Grace over to the corner of the store and lowers his voice. 'You know deep down it's not true. You must know.'

'I don't know anything right now. Between the two of you, I can't even think straight. I need you both to leave me alone. I just want some time so I can figure this all out. I need you to give me that, some time.'

'Only if you promise not to listen to any more of her lies in the meantime and not let her get inside your head any more than she already has,' says Robert pleadingly. He doesn't like the idea of knowing Eva could come back in here any time and spin her more lies.

'Just give me a couple of weeks,' says Grace. 'I want to believe you, of course I do, but you did say you were leaving her, and you clearly haven't.'

'Only because she asked me to give her a few weeks. Now I know the real reason she wanted me to stay, so she could mess with your head and get you to change your mind. I hope you don't let her succeed.'

Robert feels like his world has turned upside down thinking about a future without Grace. 'What if I leave tonight? Tell her that I won't give her the few weeks and just go?'

'No, don't that,' says Grace quickly. 'You'll just make things worse. Give her a few weeks and we'll talk then.'

Robert doesn't want to give Eva a few weeks. He doesn't want to have to be around her anymore.

'Okay,' is all he can manage to get out and leaves the store feeling defeated. He doesn't even see the car coming around the corner when he crosses the road. The one that knocks him off his feet and into the air before everything goes quiet and black.

*

The screeching of brakes and tyres outside, followed by a bang that reverberates through Grace's entire body, brings her out of the trance she'd slipped into when Robert turned away to leave.

She runs out of the store, her heart beating in her ears and her mind racing. She pushes through the crowd of people that have quickly gathered. There, in the middle of the road, Robert lays with a pool of blood around his head. Grace struggles to focus her eyes, spots forming in front of them like when you stare at a bright light too long. She can't hold it in any longer. She vomits right there and struggles to hold herself up when someone behind catches hold of her. Mr Crawford tries to console her, but she can't hear a word. Everything sounds muffled and far away. She feels herself being carried away and seated on a bench, the sound of her own screaming ringing in her ears.

*

Grace wakes the next morning in her dark bedroom feeling groggy and stiff. She can't remember how she got there, and, for a second, she forgets what happened yesterday, until the image of Robert lying in a pool of his own blood sends her head spinning. The doctors said Robert had died instantly; there was nothing anyone could have done. She'll always regret that their last conversation was her telling him she couldn't see him anymore, even though she knows deep down that he was right and Eva was lying.

Mr Crawford called Grace's sister, Ruth, yesterday. He didn't think she should go home alone. Ruth taps on the bedroom gently and opens it with a cup of tea in her hand.

'Morning, how are you feeling? Did you sleep okay?'

'I don't even remember getting home,' says Grace, her throat sore and her voice raspy from yesterday.

'The doctor gave you something to knock you out, I think.'

Ruth sits down next to Grace on the bed.

'It's in the newspapers this morning,' she says, 'about Robert. Husband of Actress Eva Taylor Killed in Hit and Run.'

'It was a hit and run?' asks Grace, eyes wide and filling with tears again.

'That's what it says. I thought you knew that. I'm so sorry, Grace,' says Ruth, wrapping her arms gently around her sister. 'I can stay as long as you need me to, okay?'

'Thank you,' says Grace, grateful for her sister. 'Do the police have any idea who did it?'

'I don't think so, not yet anyway. I'm sure they'll find them though. Don't worry about that right now. Just get some rest, okay?'

Ruth kisses Grace's forehead, just like she used to when they were younger, and Grace was ill. She was always taking care of her and always knew how to make Grace feel better. Grace lays back down and allows herself to fall into another deep sleep, away from the reality she doesn't want to think about.

*

When Grace wakes next, it must be lunch time. Despite what's happened and the nausea she's felt since hearing that awful noise yesterday, she wakes with a hungry ache in her stomach. The smell of bacon makes its way through the gap in the doorway, her stomach rumbling in response.

She sits up slowly, still weak and groggy from the sedatives and yesterday's events. She still can't make sense of what happened. Was it really a hit-and-run? Who would even do that? Eva doesn't drive; otherwise, she would be suspect number one. It must have been an accident. Robert doesn't really seem the type to upset anyone, not including herself, but that was Eva's doing. Grace wishes they hadn't ended things the way they did. She regrets not telling him she loved him too, but he must have known that she did. She hopes he knew that.

Ruth pops her head around the door again.

'Hey, do you want some bacon sandwiches? I'm making some now.'

She feels guilty for being able to think about eating, but she can't resist. 'Just one please.'

'Mr Crawford popped over this morning on his way to work. He wanted to know how you were. He said to take the next two weeks off to rest.'

'That's really kind, but I think maybe I'll just take the one week. I'd prefer the distraction.'

'But going back to where it happened after only a week might be too soon,' says Ruth.

'I'll be fine, honestly.' It's hard to sound convincing when she gets choked up every time she thinks about Robert.

'I'm going to get back to the bacon before it burns. Shall I bring it up here?'

'Yes, please.' She can't face getting out of bed yet. She's not even sure her legs could hold her weight right now; her body feels numb all over.

When Ruth returns with Grace's sandwich, she brings hers too, and they sit in bed together to eat.

'Thanks for being here, Ruth.'

'Of course,' says Ruth with a smile. 'That's what big sisters are for.'

They eat their sandwiches in silence, Ruth letting Grace lean on her for support.

*

Isabelle has been with Eva since last night, since she heard the news about Robert. Eva's still in shock, guilt settling in the pit of her stomach about how everything has turned out. Her problems involving her marriage are solved, but now Robert is dead. Despite how things had turned out, she was truly in love with him when they first met and adored him for so long. She still liked having him around, no matter how far they had drifted apart. It doesn't make sense to her that he's not here anymore.

Isabelle has already got coffee on when Eva gets up.

'I was going to make you breakfast in bed. How are you feeling today?'

'I don't know,' says Eva, standing in the doorway, looking lost. 'I don't understand what happened. The police said they had a witness to the hit-and-run. A young mother had to step back onto the pavement when a blue car came speeding down the street. That makes it sound like it was intentional, don't you think?'

'I don't know, honey,' replies Isabelle without looking up from the breakfast she's cooking. 'Just leave all that to the police. I'm sure they'll find the guy who did it.'

'I guess you're right.'

'Take a seat. Do you think you could eat something?'

'I don't know if I'm hungry or not. I feel numb and a little nauseous and dizzy,' says Eva, taking a seat at the kitchen table.

'Some food might help with that, so try to eat if you can,' says Isabelle, placing a full plate on the table in front of her. 'You hardly ate anything yesterday, remember.'

'I'll try a little. I want this turning in my stomach to stop.'

Isabelle joins Eva at the table.

'After we've eaten this, I'll pop to the shop and pick up some more groceries. I'm staying over again tonight. I'm not leaving you alone.'

'What about work?' asks Eva.

'It'll be fine. I've already spoken to my boss, and my car is in for repairs until tomorrow anyway. You know I hate travelling on the bus.'

*

A couple of weeks later, there's a big funeral. Robert was a popular guy and well respected at work. Eva doesn't see Grace there, but she didn't think she would have the guts to turn up. She's grateful for that, at least.

Isabelle has moved some of her stuff into Eva's home for now. Maybe they'll make it more permanent. Two friends living together wouldn't be suspicious at all, especially given the circumstances.

Eva's trying to be positive and look to the future now, without Robert. Who knew she still loved him so much? She didn't, not until he was gone. She heard that Grace has gone back to work, but at her boss's other store on the other side of town. She doesn't blame her. She wouldn't want to return to the scene every day either.

Isabelle insisted on getting rid of the painting Robert had bought for Eva. She said Eva looked sad every time she was looking at it, and something about it spooked her, though she wasn't sure what. She took it to a second-hand store, despite Eva insisting she wanted to keep it.

Isabelle is all Eva has now, and it's for that reason Eva tries to ignore Isabelle's growing jealousy of Robert before he died and the fact that she has a blue car that went in for repairs the evening of the accident. Eva's not strong enough to go through this alone; she needs Isabelle. So she tries to push the thoughts away every night as she lies awake next to her, locking it all in the back of her mind. For now.

Clara

Eva had been Clara's first choice to go when she first arrived at their home. Eva was selfish and treated Rob like a toy she could play with when she was bored or lonely and then toss aside when she was done. Clara knew that Robert's death would cause the most heartache.

Eva would appear fine on the surface, obviously, but it would torment her forever knowing that Isabelle had killed Robert and she had stayed with her anyway. Maybe she wasn't as strong and independent as she tried to appear to everyone. Grace was devastated for quite some time, though she did slowly begin to put her life back together. Isabelle felt no remorse for what she did. Clara knew immediately that there was a dark side to her. If anything, she seemed to enjoy hitting Robert with her car. It didn't take a whole lot of manipulation from Clara, as the willingness was already there.

Clara began to see changes in the women of the world today compared to when she was alive. They were getting stronger, wanting and demanding more for themselves than serving their husband and taking care of the children and the home like it had always been before. She thought she would have been better suited to living in these times, that maybe life would have been a little easier for her. As time moved forward, the world kept changing; sometimes the changes were subtle, sometimes they were more noticeable and occurred in a short period of time. She witnessed things she could never have imagined when she was alive.

A lot of the changes she believed were for the better. Women's fashion was one of them. She often imagined herself wearing the shorter dresses and new hairstyles that she found strange but fascinating. Women had adopted a more casual and practical way of dressing. Though Clara was enjoying watching the world change, her mind couldn't help being drawn back to her farm and her parents and her life before everything fell apart.

The next home she found herself in belonged to a young girl named Ella, who's life quickly spiralled into chaos after a dark family secret came to light. This was the first time Clara ever let someone get into her heart, bringing back feelings that she hadn't felt in so long, like compassion for another person, and wanting everything to turn out okay for them.

She began to think more of Jack and the day they met. She was walking back from the shops on a busy autumn day. The wind was picking up, and she was struggling against oncoming gusts while trying to control the long skirt of her dress from dragging her backwards and also fighting to hold on to her shopping bag. Her hat, which she left behind, had been lost to the force of the wind. Jack came running up to her, holding out her hat. He had picked it up from the roadside for her and was gesturing for her to let him carry her bag.

'Let me take that for you,' he said with a charming but nervous smile.

Clara was too flustered from the wind to turn down the offer of help, so she thanked him and handed her bag over to this stranger with chocolatey brown hair and eyes. He still looked tall despite leaning into the wind. He told Clara he was new to the town and lived with his parents and sister. He worked on a small local farm and looked pleasantly surprised when she told him that was her dream job. She fell for him instantly, and she thought he felt the same. Maybe at the time he did, but maybe he didn't want forever like she did. Clara had buried these memories for a long time, but she couldn't stop that one from coming back to haunt her. Only it didn't haunt her thinking about it now; it felt like a moment of happiness from a different life. As hard as it was to remember the bad stuff, she had forgotten that there were many good times before that too.

Ella

It's been just over two days since Ella took the crumpled-up piece of paper out of her friend Becky's bedroom bin. Ella thought Becky might regret throwing out the letter her mother left for her when she walked out over a year ago, so she decided to hold on to it for a while. In the letter, Becky's mother, Claire, blamed her husband, Martin, for her sudden departure. Martin was never physically abusive towards her, but mentally and emotionally he had worn her down with his unpredictable temper and spite. Claire had apologised in her letter for leaving Becky, but said she thought it was for the best. Becky couldn't forgive her, and Ella couldn't blame her.

Becky was having a clearout of what was left of her mother's belongings, encouraged by Martin. There was a lot she wasn't ready to let go of, but Martin has been determined to turn Becky against Claire since she left, injecting as much poison about her into Becky as he can. Ella can see how sad Becky still is about it all and how much she hopes her mother will return. She hasn't been the same since she left, but she never wants to talk about it.

Ella was only trying to help, but now she wishes she had left the letter in Becky's bin. When she took the letter home and smoothed it out as much as she could, something about the handwriting caught her eye. She took out a couple of old birthday cards from the collection she has acquired over the years and keeps on the top shelf of her wardrobe. When she compared the cards from Claire to the letter, the handwriting didn't quite match up. She's surprised Becky didn't notice but assumed she wasn't thinking straight at the time. Now Ella doesn't know whether to tell somebody or whether she's just overthinking it all. She contemplates telling her friend, Mattie, who she met on their first day at school. She knows she can trust him with anything and can also trust him to tell her when she's being stupid.

Ella sits on her bed with the letter in her hands, wondering what to do. She looks up at the painting on her bedroom wall that Becky had given her during her clearout. The painting belonged to Claire, but Becky had hung it on her bedroom wall after Martin said he didn't want it in the living room anymore. He said there was something creepy about it, even though it was just a nice painting of a family playing on a beach. Whenever Claire came into Becky's room, Ella had noticed how Claire struggled to keep her eyes off the painting, gazing at it like she was somewhere else for a moment. Ella found it fascinating how an ordinary painting had such opposing effects on Martin and Claire. It's been hanging up in her bedroom since Becky gave it to her.

Ella's at home alone today as her parents, Lucy and Daniel, and her older sister, Carrie, are working at the small grocery store her parents own near town. Ella does the odd shift here and there, but she'll be starting college after the summer. Mattie is coming over this morning to hang out, so she gets dressed and takes the letter downstairs with her, ready to show him. She can't keep it to herself any longer. She can't shake the horrible suspicion that something may have happened to Claire or that Martin may have been involved in some way. When she lets her thoughts run wild, she feels goosebumps spreading all over her arms.

She puts the kettle on ready, and Mattie arrives two minutes later.

'Hey, good timing. Just put the kettle on.'

'Great, it'll warm me up,' says Mattie, rubbing his hands together for warmth. 'It's cold this morning.'

Mattie follows Ella into the kitchen and takes a seat at the table.

'Everyone at the shop, are they?' he asks as Ella finishes making their tea.

'Yeah, I've got the house to myself this morning, which is perfect because I need to tell you something.'

'Okay. I should warn you though, I'm not open to marriage just yet. I'm way too young,' he jokes.

'Haha, you're so funny,' replies Ella sarcastically. 'It's nothing like that, but it is really serious, or I think it could be anyway.'

'Okay, pass the biscuits. You've got my attention,' he replies.

Ella joins him at the table with the tea and biscuits, and the room suddenly goes dark as the sun is blocked by a large dark cloud. Typical British weather. Mattie looks at her expectantly, like a dog waiting for their ball to be thrown.

'Okay, first you have to promise that you won't tell anyone else about this.'

'Okay, I won't tell anyone,' he says slowly, concern creeping into his voice.

'So, I was at Becky's the other day, and she was clearing out some of Claire's stuff. Remember the letter Claire wrote for her when she left? Becky threw it in the bin, and when she left the room, I took it out of the bin and put it in my pocket.'

'Why?'

'Because I thought she might end up regretting it. I was going to keep it safe for a while, in case she wanted it back.'

'Did she find out you took it?'

'I don't think so, she hasn't mentioned it anyway. The thing is, when I looked at the letter, I realised that the writing doesn't look like Claire's.'

Mattie thinks for a second, taking in what Ella's saying.

'Well, she was probably rushing,' he says, 'so it might look different. How do you know it's not the same?'

'I keep all my birthday cards, remember? So I have some from Claire and Martin; Claire always wrote in them. I used to say how neat her writing was, and I liked the way she did the loops on some of the letters. It's all different in this letter though.' She takes it out of her pocket and hands it over to Mattie. She runs upstairs quickly to dig out one of the old birthday cards to show him so he can compare. 'See what I mean? It's similar, like someone's tried to copy it but they've not done a very good job.'

'I see what you mean, yeah,' he says, holding the letter and the birthday card in front of him, his eyes flicking back and forth between the two. 'How come Becky hasn't noticed though? Surely she'd know.'

'I don't know. I think she only really read it once and then hid it away in a drawer. Maybe it was too upsetting for her to look at? Unless she has suspicions but doesn't want to admit it. Would you want to consider that your father may have killed your mother?'

Mattie puts the letter and the card down on the table and looks at her seriously, leaning his face in closer to hers.

'Have you been reading too many thrillers again?'

'Mattie, don't joke. I'm serious. It's weird, right?'

'I mean, yeah, but that's a pretty big accusation to make. I thought you meant something like she left without a word, so Martin wrote it to try and ease the blow for Becky. Murder? I don't know, that seems a bit extreme.'

'Maybe, but he is a bit odd though, isn't he? When you think about it? He's very quiet, keeps to himself, and doesn't really bother with anyone. He wasn't very nice to Claire, everyone knows that. He was always shouting at her, belittling her, always angry about something. Maybe he snapped one day, went too far.'

Mattie sits back on the sofa, contemplating what Ella's just said.

'I suppose it's not an impossible theory,' he says eventually. 'What did you want to do about it though? What can we do apart from tell someone?'

Ella sinks back a little into the sofa, slightly relieved that Mattie seems to be on the same wavelength as her now and doesn't think she's completely crazy.

'I don't really want to tell anyone else about it yet, especially Becky. I probably won't see much of her over the next couple of weeks anyway. Her gran had that fall, didn't she? She's out of hospital now so Becky's gone to stay with her to help her out for a bit until she's back on her feet properly. Also, I get the feeling she's been avoiding me lately, but I don't know, she just seems a bit off. She doesn't want to hang out as much, and she got rid of that painting too, the one that Claire loved.'

'You did say Martin is weird about Claire, like always talking badly about her to Becky and pressuring her to get rid of Claire's stuff.'

'So what do I think I should do? I can't tell anyone, but I can't go over there now because Becky's not there.'

'Yeah, that's a tough one,' says Mattie and they both stare at nothing, trying to think of a solution to this problem. 'What about that park behind their house?'

'What about it?' asks Ella.

'Their back gate runs onto the edge of the park, doesn't it? We could hang out there and see if anyone is coming or going.'

'I'm not sure that would achieve anything, to be honest. Martin doesn't seem to bother with anyone,' says Ella.

Mattie leans forward again, getting as swept up in this as Ella is.

'Didn't you say that Becky mentioned she thought Martin was seeing someone else and that's why Claire left?'

'Yeah, but she hasn't mentioned it since so I assumed it wasn't true.'

'Maybe it was. Maybe he's still seeing her?'

'Maybe,' says Ella, trying to make sense of all these little bits of information, wishing she could piece them all together and work out what's going on. 'No harm in going and watching for a little while, I guess.'

'Yeah, might be worth a shot, right? Shall we go tomorrow? We can take Charlie with us so it doesn't look like we're up to something.' Charlie is Mattie's dog, a sweet little King Charles cavalier with lots of energy.

'Sounds like a plan,' agrees Ella. 'We can make a day of it. I'll bring some food and drinks.'

'Okay, sorted,' says Mattie, getting up off the sofa and stretching. 'I've got to go. You'd better hide that letter for now, Nancy Drew.'

'If I'm Nancy Drew, who are you? Sherlock Holmes?'

'Nah, I'm not that clever. Or am I?' he says, raising one eyebrow dramatically and laughing wickedly as he gets to the front door. Ella laughs, forgetting the seriousness of the situation for a second.

'Well, we'll see tomorrow,' she says.

*

Ella's woken up by the sound of her sister, Carrie, closing the bathroom door a little too loudly, as she does every morning, and turning on the shower. Their mother, Lucy, pops her head around the door.

'You awake?' she asks, turning the light on.

'I am now,' replies Ella, squinting and shielding her eyes.

'I need you to get up early today,' says Lucy. 'I've got Amy dropping off my Avon, but I don't know what time.'

Ella sits up in bed, her eyes adjusting to the light.

'I told Mattie I'd meet him in a bit, Mam,' she says, frustrated that her mother always assumes she has no plans of her own.

'You can still go after Amy's been,' replies Lucy as she

collects a pile of washing from the chair by Ella's dressing table and puts it in the washing basket she's resting on her hip.

'It's just Avon, Mam. Can't I pick it up later?'

'No, she's going away today, so she wants everyone's orders delivered before she goes. She told me it would be early in the morning, so you'll still have plenty of time to go out.'

'Okay, fine,' sighs Ella. 'You'd better tell Carrie to hurry up in the bathroom then because I need to go in there before I come down.'

'She won't be long, she's working in the shop today. I've got to pop out to see the accountant at lunchtime so she's helping your dad out.' Lucy pauses in the doorway, frowning at the painting on Ella's wall that once belonged to Claire. 'Why do you like that painting? It's a bit boring, isn't it?'

'I like it. It was Claire's.'

'I know, but it seems a bit weird having it here, don't you think? Didn't Becky want it?'

'Not really. Well, Martin didn't want it or anything else that belonged to Claire. I think she gave it to me because she knew she'd still get to see it sometimes.'

Lucy's already stepping out of the bedroom before Ella finishes her sentence, losing interest in the conversation.

'I'll drop these at the laundrette on my way and pick them up later,' she says, before yelling at Carrie to hurry up in the bathroom so Ella can use it.

Ella looks over to the window and sees the sun trying to push through the grey clouds. She's hoping it'll brighten up for the park later.

Carrie finally emerges from the bathroom, walking into Ella's room and straight over to her dressing table.

'Can I borrow some hairspray?' she asks. 'I've run out, I'll get some in the shop later.'

'Yeah, I hardly use it anyway.'

'Thanks, I'll put it back when I'm done.' She turns around and looks at Ella still in bed. 'You'd better get up, mind. Mam's panicking about missing her Avon today. Talk about overreacting.'

She rolls her eyes and smiles at Ella as she leaves the room and heads to her own. Carrie is nineteen, three years older than Ella, and they get on quite well most of the time. Carrie likes to play the overprotective big sister when it's needed. Ella considered telling her about the letter, but she didn't know if she could trust her not to tell their parents. Mattie is the most trustworthy person Ella knows.

*

Ella sits at the kitchen table with Carrie eating her cereal, hoping that Amy will arrive before Mattie does. She also just wants to get it over with because Amy is hard to talk to. She tends to insult everyone she speaks to, particularly people she's trying to sell products to, hoping that the insults will lead to them buying some miracle cure from her to fix the part of their body she's pointed out a problem with. The last time she was over, she pointed out the dark circles under Ella's eyes before asking if she'd seen the new serum Avon had just started selling that could get rid of those instantly. Ella mumbled something about being up late the night before and tried to ignore her comments.

'I hope Amy isn't going to expect to be invited in today, Mam. I can't be dealing with her insults today,' says Ella as Lucy is getting ready to leave.

'No, she'll be in a rush today,' she replies, checking the contents of her handbag and putting her jacket on. 'Just nod along anyway. That's what the rest of us do. Just tell her you'll have a look at the brochure for next time.'

'So you do notice what she's like then?'

'Everyone does, love, but she sells some nice stuff so we tolerate her.'

Carrie looks at Ella and rolls her eyes again before getting up to rinse her bowl and getting ready to leave.

'Enjoy your day,' she grins. 'Don't go buying anything you don't want.'

'Very funny. Maybe I'll tell her you'd like a chat next time she's around so you can find out what new products she's selling.'

'Don't you dare,' says Carrie seriously.

Five minutes later, everyone has rushed off, leaving Ella to get some sandwiches and snacks ready for her and Mattie for the park. She runs upstairs to brush her teeth, and grabs a pair of faded blue jeans and a plain green t-shirt. She runs back downstairs after brushing her straight, light brown hair and applying a coat of mascara and a little blush to her cheeks.

Amy arrives not much later, knocking loudly on the door. A loud knock to match her loud personality. Ella quickly rushes to the door, eager to get this all over with.

'Hi Ella,' says Amy in her high-pitched, cheery voice. 'Did your mam tell you I was dropping these off today?'

'Yeah, I've got the money here for you,' says Ella, handing her the money Lucy left on the sideboard. Amy hands her the bag and counts the money to check the amount.

'Did you think anymore about that eye serum I suggested, love?' she says, without even looking up from the cash in her hand.

'Well…'

'You still look a bit peaky.' Amy examines Ella's face a little too closely for Ella's liking.

'I'm just a bit tired this morning. I'll take a look at the next brochure.'

'Okay, well, I've got to run, so tell your mam I'll see her when I get back.'

'Okay, enjoy your holiday,' says Ella as politely as she can manage.

'Thanks, love.'

Ella shuts the door and checks the time. Mattie should be here any minute now.

*

The sandwiches and snacks are all ready in Ella's bag, and Charlie is eager to get going when Mattie puts his lead back on. It's just a five-minute walk to the park, less if Charlie has anything to do with it.

'I hope you're prepared for a long day,' says Mattie. 'You know we probably won't find anything out from one day watching the back of their house.'

'I know,' replies Ella, trying to keep up as Charlie pulls Mattie along eagerly. 'At least it's not raining.'

'Yeah, I draw the line at hanging out in the rain all day, just so you know. You might get more luck if you actually spend more time at Becky's instead of her going to yours most of the time.'

'I know, I was thinking that too. She's with her gran for a couple of weeks now, though.'

They sit on a bench under a tall oak tree, the shade making Ella pull her jacket a little tighter around herself.

'I'll take the ball and play with Charlie for a bit while you keep an eye on the house. It might warm me up a bit,' says Ella.

'Okay. You can borrow my jacket though if you want. I'm not that cold.'

'Nah, it's fine. It's nice to spend some time with Charlie.' Ella's parents had never let them have a dog. They said they were too busy with the shop and it would be left alone too much. She knows they had a point, but she thought they might have changed their minds when Ella and Carrie were older and could help look after it. They both offered to do their bit, but their parents wouldn't budge, especially their mother.

Ella goes over to the large grassy area with Charlie, throwing the ball for him, which he brings back enthusiastically. After running around with him for a while, she almost forgets why she's there. She unzips her jacket and takes it over to the bench, where Mattie still sits with his eyes on the back of Becky and Martin's house.

'You can have a rest now, mind,' he says, taking in her flushed face. 'Charlie won't mind, will you, Charlie?' He makes a fuss of the dog who's panting loudly.

'Okay, but just to give Charlie a rest.'

'Yeah, yeah. Just admit you're knackered,' says Mattie, looking amused.

'Maybe a bit, but he does look like he needs a drink.' She sits on the bench next to Mattie, rummaging through her bag for a drink. 'Seen anything yet?'

'Nope,' he says, busying himself with getting a drink for Charlie and avoiding eye contact.

'Why are you lying?'

'What? I'm not,' he says adamantly.

'I know you, Mattie, and I can tell when you're hiding something.'

He sighs and looks at her.

'I don't want to say. It's probably nothing.'

'Then tell me,' she says, attracting a little attention from an elderly couple walking on the path not too far from them with her slightly raised voice.

'Okay. About five minutes ago, I saw your mother going in the back gate to Becky's house.'

Ella's mouth falls open slightly, but no words come out.

'She looked around first,' continues Mattie, 'but she didn't look over this way. I doubt she saw you over there with Charlie. Like I said, though, it's probably nothing.'

'I don't understand,' says Ella, trying to piece the story together in her head. 'She told us she was going to see the accountant today. If it's nothing, why would she lie about it? Why would she be going to see Martin anyway?'

'I don't know, Ella.' Mattie movies closer, placing a comforting hand on top of hers. 'It could be anything. We shouldn't jump to conclusions yet.'

It's too late though. Ella's mind is playing out so many different scenarios, none of them good.

'You must have thought there was something to it. You didn't want to tell me,' she says.

Mattie tries to relax his voice and his posture.

'I was just surprised, I guess. I didn't expect to see her there. What do you want to do?'

'Wait until she comes out,' says Ella quickly. 'See how long she stays.'

'Okay, but if she goes out the front, we won't see her leave.'

'I doubt she will. She wouldn't sneak in the back to leave out the front door.'

Mattie can see that Ella is trying to hide how upset she is, trying to avoid eye contact with him, staring intently at the back gate of Becky's house.

'Maybe she's gone to see Becky about something,' Mattie offers gently.

'Becky's not there, remember? She's with her gran.'

In the silence that follows, it really sinks in for Ella that her mother might be hiding something. So many thoughts are spinning around in her head that she can't make sense of any of them. Mattie puts a comforting arm around her.

'I'm sorry, Ella. Maybe coming here was a bad idea.'

'Do you think she could be cheating on my dad with Martin?' she asks abruptly.

Mattie hesitates before shrugging slightly and looking away from her.

'I don't know,' he says. 'I'd find it hard to believe, though. Your mam and dad always seem happy together, don't they? It wouldn't make sense really, but then I suppose affairs never do. Are you going to say anything to her?'

'I don't know.' Ella pauses, her mind still running wild, horrified at the words that are about to come out of her mouth. 'Do you think if they have been having an affair, that Martin could have killed Claire to get her out of the way? Maybe she found out?'

Martin takes a long breath out, contemplating what Ella's just asked him.

'I don't know. Sounds a bit mental when you say it out loud, doesn't it? Like something from a book or a film. I hope nothing happened to Claire. We could be way off the mark with all this. Don't go getting ahead of yourself now until we know more. If you accuse your mother and you're wrong, imagine how that would go down.'

'I know, but how am I supposed to act like nothing's wrong? This will drive me crazy until I know exactly what's going on.'

Ella looks away, trying to figure out how to handle what feels like an impossible dilemma.

'Look,' says Mattie, tapping her arm and pointing to the house. They watch Becky go through her back gate, then sit and wait. Less than two minutes later, Lucy rushes through the gate, closes it behind her, and then pauses. She reaches for something in her bag, then dabs at her eyes with a tissue, trying not to mess up her make-up. That's when Ella realises that she always wears more make-up on days she has an appointment with the accountant. Her dad has joked about it a couple of times lately. Lucy stands up tall and takes a deep breath. For a second, Ella thinks she looks straight at her and Mattie, but she turns and walks away briskly.

'I think I'm right. I think she's seeing Martin. Thinking about little things now, it does kind of make sense.'

'I'm so sorry, Ella. Do you want to come to my house for a while? Think we're done here for the day and you're shivering.'

She's already up on her feet, ready to leave.

*

Mattie and Ella spend the rest of the afternoon listening to music in Mattie's room, with Charlie curled up on the floor by the bed.

'Do you want to stay over tonight?' asks Mattie, concerned that Ella might not want to go home or that she might confront her mother before knowing everything.

Ella gladly takes him up on the offer; she's not ready to face her mother yet. She knows Lucy has the day off work tomorrow. Lucy always has Wednesdays off and tells them all that she's popping to town to do some shopping. Now Ella is wondering what lies she has fallen for over the last year or so. Does she really go to town? Ella can't help but question everything at this point. Mattie nips over to the shop to grab some popcorn for them to watch a movie together and to let Lucy know that Ella will be staying at his house for the night. Both of their parents are fine with Ella staying over. She's fallen asleep there many times. Mattie has a black and white TV in his bedroom. Most people just have the one TV downstairs, so Ella likes that they can watch films together in peace without having to sit with their parents. Ella asked if she could have one in her bedroom before, but her parents told her they couldn't afford such luxuries.

'Did she say anything?' asks Ella when Mattie returns.

'Not really. She asked why you didn't go over with me though.'

'What did you say?'

'I just said you were tired after being out all day,' he shrugs.

'Did she seem off at all? Do you think she saw us?'

'I don't think so,' says Mattie, although he doesn't sound convinced. 'She seemed like normal, I think.'

He gently moves Charlie over a little, who's curled up next to Ella on the bed, and places a bowl of popcorn down before sitting with her.

'Okay. Thanks for letting me stay over. I just want to try to forget about it tonight.'

'Sounds like a good idea,' he says. 'You know you're always welcome to stay here for a few days if things get bad. My parents won't mind.'

'Thanks. I might need to take you up on that,' she says, reaching for the popcorn. That's the last they speak about it all night, but one thing was playing on Ella's mind that she couldn't stop thinking about. What happened earlier when Becky got back? What does she know?

*

Ella feels like she blinked and the night disappeared. She slept surprisingly well, although she always does here. Her thoughts quietened while watching the movie with Mattie, and she had fallen asleep before it ended. She turns to find herself alone in the room, the smell of cooking bacon drifting through the door. Cathy, Mattie's mother, is always happy to cook for Mattie and his friends. Ella loves coming here for food. Mattie walks through the door with two plates of egg and bacon sandwiches. Ella can't help thinking about what a great husband Mattie will make some day, but quickly shakes that thought out of her head and tucks into her sandwich.

'Do you want me to come over with you this morning?' says Mattie, glancing up at her and trying to work out how she's feeling after sleeping on everything.

'I'm okay, thanks. Think I should probably speak to my mother alone.'

'You are going to speak to her then?'

'I think I have to. I can't just forget about it, can I?'

'Let me know how it goes though, yeah? Or I'll be worrying about you all day.'

'I know, I will,' says Ella, giving him a reassuring smile.

'You're dribbling butter all down your chin, by the way,' says Mattie, smirking as he hands her a box of tissues.

'I can't help it. It's all melted,' she says, managing to catch a bit of butter from falling onto her top.

'Yeah, but you don't see me dribbling.'

'That's because your mouth is too big to miss anything.' She jokingly tosses the tissue box back at him, and they laugh, giving Ella a moment to forget what she's going back home to.

*

After breakfast, Ella gathers her things together and puts her boots on.

'I'm just going to go now and get this over with,' she says, scanning the room to check she hasn't forgotten anything. 'I'll call around later, shall I?'

'Yeah, cool. Any time is fine.'

Ella leaves before she can change her mind, walking home a little too quickly, not giving herself enough time to plan how to approach this or what she should say before she arrives at her front door. Her hand shakes slightly as she puts the key in the door and pushes it open. She's never had to confront her mother over anything. They've always had quite a good relationship, never arguing like some of her friends do with their mothers.

'Is that you, Ella?' Lucy's voice calls from the kitchen.

Ella clears her throat. 'Yeah, it's me.'

'I'm just making tea. I'll bring it in the living room now. Do you want some biscuits?'

Lucy's voice is at a higher pitch than normal, the house vibrating with nervous tension.

'No thanks, just tea is fine.'

Ella sits down on the armchair opposite the sofa where Lucy always sits. She wants to be able to take in her facial expressions and her body language, in case she tries to lie to her about anything. Lucy enters the living room carrying two cups, steam rising from them both into the air.

'You okay? Did you and Mattie enjoy your film last night?' Lucy keeps her focus on the tea, not looking at Ella at all.

'Yeah, it was okay.'

Lucy sits opposite Ella, looking at her for the first time. She seems fidgety, like she doesn't know what to do with her hands. She leans forward and picks up her tea, giving them something to do.

They sit in silence for a moment, neither of them knowing how to begin what will surely be an uncomfortable conversation. Ella opens her mouth, even though she doesn't know what to say, but Lucy speaks first.

'I know you saw me leaving Becky's house yesterday. I saw you and Mattie at the park. That's why you stayed at Mattie's, isn't it?'

Ella's taken aback that Lucy has brought it up first, but now she feels like she has the opening she needed to ask all the questions flying around in her head.

'Yeah, it is. What's going on? Are you seeing Martin? I saw

Becky going in. Did she catch you both?' Ella takes a breath, trying to stop every question coming out in one go, giving her mother a minute to answer. Lucy's eyes fill with tears, and her hand trembles so much she has to place her mug back down on the coffee table.

'I'm so sorry, love,' she says, her voice shaking. 'Please don't tell your dad. I went there yesterday to tell Martin it was over, I promise.' She moves towards Ella, but Ella stands up to put the distance back between them.

'I can't believe it's true,' she says, half-expecting there to have been some reasonable explanation for everything, to feel stupid but relieved that she was wrong. 'How could you do that? He was so horrible to Claire, and Claire was your friend, remember? How long has it been going on?'

'About two years,' she says quietly, unable to look Ella in the eye.

'So before Claire supposedly left, then?'

'Supposedly?' asks Lucy, her eyes widening slightly as she looks directly at Ella.

Ella was right about the affair. Now she's convinced she must be right about all of it. She feels no need to hold back on any of her suspicions now.

'I know Claire didn't write that letter to Becky. It's not her handwriting. It was Martin, wasn't it? What did he do to her? What did he tell you?'

Lucy moves towards Ella, but she quickly moves away from her again, sitting on the opposite end of the sofa to where Lucy had just sat.

'Ella, slow down. You're getting ahead of yourself now. He didn't do anything to Claire. She just left, like he said. I can't explain the letter. Maybe he wrote it to make Becky feel better?'

'Maybe I'll go over there and ask him then, shall I?' says Ella, staring intently at Lucy, watching for signs of her cracking.

'Don't do that,' she replies quietly. 'Becky doesn't know anything, and he wants to keep it that way. So do I.'

'But you were there yesterday when Becky was there.'

'I just said I was dropping something off that he left at the shop.'

Ella considers what Lucy is telling her, that Claire leaving was her own choice, but something doesn't sit right with Ella. She can't let go of the idea that something might have happened to her. Lucy continues to plead her case, noticing Ella's uncertainty about Martin and Claire.

'He wouldn't hurt her, Ella. He wouldn't hurt anyone, let alone kill them, if that's what you're getting at.' She lets her weight fall into the armchair, exhausted by the whole situation.

Ella shakes her head decidedly; she can't accept what Lucy is saying. Martin wouldn't hurt anyone? He was fine with Becky, but how can Lucy say he wouldn't hurt anyone? He tortured Claire for years; she was miserable.

'No. I'm going over there later. I'm going to ask him what happened.'

'Please stop this, Ella,' says Lucy, getting more and more frustrated. 'You're going to tear this family apart if it comes out about us. Think about Becky, too.'

'I am thinking about Becky. You can't change my mind.'

Lucy's panic fully kicks in. She stands up and starts pacing back and forth in front of the fireplace.

'How is this going to help her? She'll just hate her dad for having an affair, and it won't bring Claire back. She'll be more alone than ever.'

'Bring Claire back from where?' says Ella, standing in front of her mother, blocking her from pacing anymore. 'Tell me where she is.'

'I don't know, Ella,' says Lucy, trying to calm her voice and return Ella's gaze. 'She just left; I don't know how many different ways to tell you.'

Ella knows she's lying. In that moment, they feel like strangers.

'Have it your way,' says Ella, turning around and storming off out of the house, grabbing her jacket on the way. She heads over to Martin's house, leaving Lucy sobbing on the sofa.

*

Ella stops at the park on her way to Martin's and sits down on one of the swings, mindlessly swinging back and forth slightly while glaring at the back of Martin's house. She needs a minute to gather her thoughts and think about what her mother said. Instead, her mind goes further back, pointing out all the signs she missed that seem so obvious now. The way she would put Ella's dad off joining her for her appointments with the accountant, telling him she could deal with that side of things, only one of them needed to go. The way she tried to avoid Carrie's offers of joining her on her Wednesday shopping trips, even though Carrie seemed like she really wanted to go and they used to go shopping together regularly.

Then there was the change in Lucy when Claire went missing. Looking back on it now, Ella remembers her being constantly on edge, always jumpy when the police were mentioned, and always trying to change the subject, despite being good friends with Claire at one point. She seemed to get back to herself a little when the police concluded that Claire had just run off, as her letter said, and there was no suspicious activity to follow up. It all seems so clear now. Ella wonders why she didn't see it all before. Maybe she didn't want to believe her mother could do anything like that. She told herself she was being silly and that it was just down to the shock of Claire leaving so suddenly.

Ella doesn't want to make the same mistakes again. She gets up and, reluctantly but determinedly, walks towards Martin's house.

*

'I know.'

Martin stands in the doorway, looking Ella up and down and glancing around her to see if there's anyone around. He grabs her arm and steers her into the living room.

'Know what?' he snarls at her, all too calmly for Ella's liking. 'What do you think you know, Ella?'

She tries to appear confident under his intimidating gaze, lifting her chin slightly.

'I know about you and my mother, to start with. I know that the letter Claire left for Becky isn't in Claire's handwriting, and I know that she didn't just leave.'

He pauses for a moment, processing what she's saying. His mouth curls at the corner into a smirk.

'I guess you know most of it then, but not quite all.'

The blood rushes to Ella's head, and she starts to feel a little dizzy. Martin gestures towards the sofa.

'You'd better sit down, Ella. You're looking a little peaky.'

Ella reluctantly moves towards the sofa. Suddenly it doesn't feel like such a good idea coming over her and confronting someone she believes could be a murderer. She glances around, planning different exit routes in case she needs to get out quick, but when she looks back at Martin, his face is serious and the coldness has gone. With a sombre look on his face, he sits down on the other end of the sofa, keeping a little distance between them. He looks down at his hands when he starts to speak again.

'So you've worked out that the letter wasn't from Claire, but I think you've got the wrong end of the stick about what actually happened. Claire was murdered, you're right about that. I hate to break it to you, but it wasn't me that did it. It was your mother.'

Even though she's sitting down, Ella feels as though the ground is moving beneath her, like when you lay down on your bed after too many drinks and the room starts spinning. He's lying, she thinks. He must be lying.

'Claire found out about us. She started attacking your mother, and your mother just lost it. Grabbed the old fire poker we used to keep there and hit her with it. She didn't stop until Claire stopped moving. Even then I had to grab her to calm her down, it was like she was possessed.'

He shakes his head, raising his hand to his forehead and taking a moment before carrying on.

'Your mother told me to get rid of the poker, but, in the state she was in, she didn't notice that I just grabbed it with a carrier bag and hid it in the kitchen cupboard, under the sink. I threatened to tell the police and give it to them if she didn't leave me and Becky alone. I didn't want her around us. I was scared for Becky. I helped her get rid of Claire's body and clean up. She still comes around sometimes, begging for my forgiveness and wanting to start things up again, but I'll never be able to get the image of what she did to Claire out of my head.'

Ella can't speak. She doesn't know what to think. She's always found Martin cold and harsh, but now it's like a different person is sitting next to her, someone broken and ashamed. Ella can't quite wrap her head around her mother doing something like that. She's not the most patient person, but she's never had a temper, never lost it like Martin describes. Martin looks so sincere, though, she doesn't know what to believe.

'I'm really sorry, Ella,' he says. 'I never wanted you or your family to find out, for your sakes. I'll get you some water.'

He heads out to the kitchen, and Ella doesn't move at all in the time he's gone. He places the glass in her shaky hands. She takes a small sip and clears her throat.

'Does Becky know about any of this?' she asks.

'No, of course not. And I hope she never will. Your mother is a dangerous person, Ella.'

She can't process any of this. She suddenly wishes Mattie was here with her.

'What are you going to do?' he asks, with the same nervousness in his voice that Lucy had earlier.

'I don't know. I don't want Becky to find out, but if things happen as you say they did, then my mother should pay for that.'

'It would tear your family apart, you know that.'

Ella's never seen this side of Martin before—a softer, caring side.

'I know. I need to think. I'm going to go see Mattie and try to clear my head.'

She places the glass of water down on the coffee table and slowly gets up from the sofa. Martin quickly gets up too.

'Will you tell him?' he asks.

'No. I don't think so. Probably not.'

'If you feel you need to tell anyone, I'll need to know. It'll affect me and Becky too,' he says, trying to remind Ella about her friend and the damage this could do if she finds out that her mother is dead.

'You'll know,' she says. The room feels smaller suddenly, the ceiling lower. She needs to get out of here. She rushes out the front door and inhales deeply, feeling like she'd been holding her breath the whole time she'd been in the house.

She rushes over to Mattie's and ends up blurting everything out to him as soon as she steps through his door.

Mattie listens with his mouth hanging half open the whole time and sits in silence for a while, too stunned to speak. After contemplating everything Ella's told him, he frowns a little.

'Are you sure he's telling the truth?'

'I don't know, but he seemed genuine. He seemed quite upset by the whole thing.'

Ella goes over every detail of her conversation with Martin, with Mattie listening intently, nodding along seriously. The more Ella talks about it and thinks about it, the more confused she is. Surely her mother wouldn't do something like that? But does anyone ever believe a loved one is capable of something like that, even with all the evidence before them? The way Martin described it was so brutal, so unlike her mother.

After another hour or so of talking things through, Mattie comes to the conclusion that all Ella can do now is speak to her mother about it.

'You can't ignore it, can you?' he says. 'It'll drive you crazy. If you talk to her about it, you can see how she reacts.'

'Yeah, I think you're right,' says Ella, still in a daze, staring off at nothing in particular.

'Want me to walk you back?'

'Would you mind?'

'Course not.'

They walk back to Ella's slowly. The air is cold, and it's starting to get dark. Ella stops outside her front door and checks the time on her watch.

'My dad and Carrie will be back soon. I think I'll have to wait until tomorrow to talk to her.'

'Looks she might not be home anyway,' says Mattie, nodding to the house. There are no lights on, but it's not that dark yet.

Ella turns her key in the lock and opens the front door. She calls out, but they are met with silence.

'Maybe she's gone to find out what happened at Martin's,' says Mattie. They walk into the living room and spot a letter on the coffee table. Ella freezes, her eyes wide. Mattie leans forward and picks up the letter. He hands it to Ella, standing next to her so they can both read it.

'Dear Dylan, I'm so sorry, but I can't take this any longer. I've not been happy for a while, and I couldn't face telling you because I didn't want to hurt you. I've decided to go away for a while. Please take good care of the girls, although I know you will. You always do. I'll be in touch when I'm settled somewhere, or maybe it's for the best that I leave you all alone for a while. I'm so sorry. Lucy.'

Ella drops the letter, letting it float to the ground, landing softly on the carpet.

'That's not my mother's handwriting. It's the same as Claire's letter.' Her whole body begins to shake, and she turns to Mattie, her eyes filled with terror. 'He was lying. It wasn't my mother, it was him.' Ella's voice becomes strangled, and she gasps for air, searching for something to lean on, to hold her up.

Mattie gently leads her over to sit down on the sofa.

'How could I be so stupid?' she says, reaching forward for the letter on the floor and scanning it once more. 'I believed every word he said about my mother without questioning it. Why would I do that?' Her eyes fill with tears. Mattie leans closer, putting an arm around her shoulder and taking her hand with his.

'You were vulnerable, and he knew it. You'd just found out she'd been having an affair, and you were already upset with her. I believed it for a moment too, Ella.'

'Do you think she's dead? Do you think this means he's killed her?' Her voice starts to rise in panic again, but Mattie's focus is elsewhere.

'I don't know,' he says. 'Maybe that'll tell us.' He points to another letter perched on the armchair, with Ella's name on it.

Mattie opens it, Ella can't bring herself to. He reads it out for her.

'Ella, I bet you're wondering what happened to your mother. Did I kill her or tell her to leave and never come back with the threat of killing her precious family? What a situation you've put us all in. What happens next is down to you now, Ella. If you try to find your mother or tell anyone what you've discovered today, I will kill her. The choice is yours. Risk your mother or risk yourself and your whole family. Choose wisely.'

'Oh my god,' says Ella, barely above a whisper. 'What do I do now?'

Mattie sighs, scratching his forehead and sitting on the coffee table, still looking at the letter for a moment.

'What can you do? You know what he's capable of now. Apart from ignoring it, anything you do will end with someone losing their life.' Mattie wants to comfort her, but he can't come up with anything comforting to do or say.

Ella sits on the sofa, her mind going a million miles an hour, before giving in and admitting that there's nothing else she can do. Martin has all the control now.

'Either way, I'm never going to see my mother again, am I?' she says sadly, the realisation sinking in.

Mattie folds the letter back into the envelope and stuffs it in his pocket.

'I think you have to drop it now before anyone else gets hurt, at least for now. I'm sorry, Ella, but this has gotten way out of hand. Right now, I don't think you should mention anything about Lucy and Martin to your family. It's too dangerous for your mother. Hide this letter for now and leave the one for your dad on the table. I don't think you have a choice for now.'

Ella knows that Mattie is right.

'I said so many horrible things to my mother. You should have seen her when I left.'

'Maybe we can figure something else out in time, but not tonight. We've already been hasty, and look where that's got us.'

She puts the letter for her dad back on the table, and they head upstairs like they've not seen or read it. She knows this is going to destroy her family.

*

Becky heard everything the day Claire found out about Martin and Lucy's affair. She heard Lucy shouting at Claire, telling her that Martin didn't want her anymore. Three voices yelling over each other, and then a loud thud, followed by another. A moment of silence before Lucy screamed in horror. 'What did you do?' Becky knew then that her mother was dead, and that her father had killed her. She realised they must not have known she was home, so she stayed silent in her bedroom while they argued over what to do about Claire's body. She heard Martin threatening to pin the blame on Lucy if she said a word to anyone, reminding her that her fingerprints were already on the fire poker. She listened to them wrapping Claire's body up and loading her into the back of Martin's van. Then, when they'd left, she ran to the bathroom and threw up into the toilet, tears streaming down her face, her whole body shaking uncontrollably.

Becky had known about Martin's and Lucy's affair for a while, but she didn't know how to tell her mother. She didn't want to hurt her. After that night, Lucy only came round out of fear of Martin telling anyone that she killed Claire.

Becky found it hard to be around Ella after it happened.

Ella seemed to put her change in behaviour down to being upset about her mother leaving, and Becky let her believe that. There was a different atmosphere between them, a new tension. Neither of them said a word about it, but they could both feel it, though only Becky understood the reason for it.

Last night, Martin told Lucy she had to leave, to disappear, and never come back. If she did, he would kill Ella and Carrie. Becky felt sick at the thought of it. She thought what happened with Claire was a brief moment of rage, that he got caught up in the moment. She thought maybe he even felt guilty afterwards, as he seemed to try so hard to take good care of Becky. But now she can see that he's just evil, and she's terrified of what he might do.

She needs to do something; he needs to be stopped. Before leaving her gran's this evening, she sneaks a bottle of whisky from the cabinet into her bag. It's been there some years now. Her grandfather used to like a tipple, as he would call it, but her gran never liked whisky, so it's been sitting in the cabinet since before he died. Becky knows nothing will wake her father with this in his system; whisky always puts him right out for the night.

She waits for him to come home from work, the whisky on the table waiting for him. They eat their tea in front of the tele in the living room, the sound of the TV making up for the lack of conversation. She struggles to get her food down, but she tries as hard as she can, taking small mouthfuls and forcing it down her throat. She doesn't want Martin to sense that anything is wrong. When his plate is clear, she quickly gets up, offering to take his plate out for him.

'Thanks, love,' he says, handing her the plate and smiling at her with love. For a moment, she reconsiders what she's about to do, but reminds herself that even though he loves her, he's a bad person who will only hurt more people if he has the chance to.

'Want a drink, Dad?' she asks, heading out to the kitchen. 'I found a bottle of whisky at Gran's today and brought it back for you.'

'Yeah, grab me a glass, will you?'

She hands him the glass quickly, trying to steady her shaking hand so that he doesn't notice, but he barely takes his eyes off the TV anyway. They sit watching TV together for a while in silence, Becky desperately hoping he'll drink enough so that nothing will wake him, keeping an eye for signs of the whisky kicking in. Soon enough, he starts wrestling to keep his eyes open, shaking his head a couple of times trying to wake himself up. He frowns and puts his glass on the table in front of him, then leans back and lets the tiredness wash over him. Becky waits a little, then slowly walks over to him, her breath quickening as she puts her face close to his for any signs of movement, her heart racing in her chest.

'Dad?' she says. 'Dad?'

He doesn't react at all, so she tries again, louder. Still no reaction. She takes a lighter out of her back pocket and lights one of the candles on the fire place. She gets her backpack that she prepared earlier, just a couple of sentimental bits that she couldn't bear to part with. Although she realised she'd have to leave most of it, otherwise people might get suspicious. With her shoes on and her backpack ready to go, she walks back into the living room. Martin is sleeping open-mouthed, his head back, dead to the world. She turns to the lit candle and knocks it to the ground. It lands in front of Martin, the flame quickly latching on to the carpet around his feet and spreading all around him. She leaves quickly and heads to her gran's house. She worries that regret and guilt might consume her at some point, but, at the moment, all she feels is relief.

Becky knows where Lucy is. Martin had sent her to an old run-down house that a friend of his owned. He wanted her to go away but wanted to know where she was so he could keep a close eye on her. When Martin's body is discovered, Becky will tell her she can go home now. She should go home as soon as possible to avoid any unwanted attention while Martin's death is being investigated. Ella and her family will be safe again.

Becky will stay with her gran for now, where she prefers to be anyway. She knows Lucy will suspect her of starting the fire, but she's never going to say anything. Like her, she'll probably want to forget everything that happened in that house anyway and get on with rebuilding her life.

Lucy asks Ella to get rid of the painting from Becky's house when she returns home. She doesn't want any reminders of what happened. Ella agrees, knowing that her mother's memories will haunt her daily for the rest of her life anyway. It's almost like Lucy believes the painting witnessed what happened to Claire and is judging her every day.

Clara

As soon as Clara discovered just how evil Martin was, she started questioning everything she had been doing. It made her think that what she was doing was no better than what he did. Even though she used other people and didn't get her own hands dirty, the decisions they made were mostly down to her.

She suddenly felt a deep hatred for who and what she had become. And for what? Because a man had wronged her. It's not like Jack was evil like Martin, just weak. She started to realise that she shouldn't have let it consume her and take over her whole life the way she did. She was never the strong woman she wanted to be, just incredibly stubborn.

She had blocked out all memories of Jack for so long, but now she couldn't seem to stop them from seeping into her mind. The good memories didn't make her feel the same way anymore. The hurt, anger, and bitterness began to fade away and were replaced by something else. Some of the memories even made her smile a little, because how could they not? They did have many good times together before everything fell apart.

Claire used to look at the painting sometimes like she was begging for help. Clara questioned later on whether she could have helped her. If she had stepped in sooner, maybe she could have saved her life. She found herself wishing she had. She read this one all wrong.

Clara laid low for a while after this one, contemplating how she should be using this power she had, wondering if she had it in her to maybe do some good instead, help people who needed it. She saw too much of a resemblance to herself in Martin's ugliness.

Maybe she could help the ones who deserved it instead, people like Claire and Ella. Clara had confined herself to eternity within the painting; she knew she had all the time she would need to learn how to be better. The only way she could be put to rest was if the painting was destroyed, but she had made it so that none of the owners could ever bring themselves to do that.

She decided that, going forward, only the people who deserved it would suffer, and she would try to help the good people who needed it. She hoped she would never come across someone like Martin again.

One day she found herself in the home of a young couple named Luke and Beth, after being confined to a cupboard under the stairs for years. Luke's parents reminded Clara of her own: loving, kind, and always there to help. Clara's parents never talked about it, but she knew they visited the daughter she gave up regularly after making arrangements with the new parents. Clara never asked, and they never brought it up. They all knew it would be too painful. The new parents named the girl Eliza, and she looked just like her mother.

Beth & Luke

Beth and Luke are in a dingy bed and breakfast. The bedding is old and faded, probably covered in a layer of dust. The walls are painted dark green, and the light bulbs are dull, giving very little light to the room. Beth has braved the bathroom, but Luke stands in the middle of the room, too disgusted to touch anything.

'What was the name of this place again?' he calls to Beth. 'Wasn't the Bates Motel, was it?'

A scream echoes from the bathroom, and his stomach drops. He thought this place had murder written all over it, but he wasn't expecting anything to actually happen. He steps towards the bathroom door, images of Beth in a blood bath flashing through his head. To his relief, Beth comes running out wrapped in a towel before he gets to the door. She continues to scream and shakes her head, running her hands through her hair. She stops and laughs hysterically when she notices the terror across Luke's face. Her hair is soaking wet, and she's splashing drops of water everywhere in her frenzy.

'Go and look at the size of that cockroach in there,' she says, her voice high-pitched. 'It was in my hair.' She shakes her hair again and her whole body. 'It feels like it's still crawling on me. I'm never going to sleep tonight.'

Luke laughs and pulls her closer.

'Well, I'll just have to stay awake and keep you company,' he says.

She smiles and wraps her arms around his neck.

'If you don't get rid of that thing, you'll be spending the night in the bathroom keeping it company.'

He sighs jokingly and nods.

'Okay, Beth,' he says. 'Anything for you.' He leans in and kisses her gently on her forehead. 'But if I don't make it out, remember you forced me into this battle.'

He picks up a newspaper off the bedside table and goes into the bathroom, stopping at the door to give a soldier's salute. Beth laughs and follows behind him.

'I want to make sure you get it,' she says.

'Trust me, I'm a pro,' he replies confidently.

After a few missed attempts and a few more screams, they both hurry back out of the bathroom, red-faced and out of breath.

'Told you I'd get it.'

'You did. You might want to hang on to that newspaper though. I don't think that'll be the last one we see tonight,' says Beth.

'Don't worry, it's only one night. We'll be home tomorrow, in our new home. My mother said she'd have everything ready for us when we get there.'

'I can't believe we actually have a home of our own,' she says, smiling so big that Luke momentarily forgets the dirty room they're in and sees only a future of happiness with Beth.

*

Beth can't sleep. Partly down to fear of waking up to cockroaches crawling all over her, partly because she's so eager to get their new home tomorrow, but mostly because she ran into her uncle, Brian, a few days ago. It was the first time she'd seen him in years. She barely even recognised him at first. They bumped into each other at the supermarket. He said he was staying in the area for a work thing, and they shared some awkward small talk before Brian dropped the bombshell that Beth's parents were planning on coming back to the country soon and had mentioned contacting Beth for a visit. She had left the shop without her groceries and ran to the car to calm her breathing, her shaky hands gripping the steering wheel. She knew that they'd probably heard about the house she and Luke had inherited from his aunt, Rose. They would probably come sniffing for handouts, assuming there might be some money left to them too. Beth started to drive home before realising she couldn't go back without her groceries; she didn't want to tell Luke what had happened. She wanted to forget about it, hoping that they would never actually turn up.

Luke knew all about her parents, but she was still embarrassed. His parents were so lovely and always went above and beyond for Luke and now Beth too.

Beth's parents had never really wanted her. She was just an inconvenience, a mistake that they had to live with. Her mother took pleasure in reminding Beth of that frequently. As soon as Beth turned sixteen, her parents moved away without telling her. They had been travelling without her since she was ten years old anyway, leaving barely enough money for food while they were gone, but this time they weren't planning on coming back. They left a brief and emotionless note to tell her they had gone to live in France.

'You're sixteen now,' her mother wrote. 'You don't need us to take care of you anymore. You can look after yourself. There's money under our mattress, enough to last you a few weeks until you get a job. It's all we can spare, so make it last. There's no more to send you.'

There wasn't enough money to last a week, so she had to find a job fast. Beth was used to taking care of herself anyway; no one else ever had. Luke knew what her parents were like; the whole town did. No one ever said anything to her, but her elderly neighbour would leave food by the front door sometimes when Beth was alone, and other people would offer sympathetic smiles and ask if there was anything she needed. Beth thinks that's why Luke is always reassuring her that he'll always take care of her. She's never doubted him.

After a restless night of tossing and turning and coughing through all the dust filling the worst bed and breakfast they've ever spent the night in, Beth and Luke still wake surprisingly happy, the excitement of getting to their new home overriding anything else. Luke's aunt, Rose, passed away a few months ago, leaving them the house and her two dogs, Ben and Scamp. The house is old and needs a lot of work, but it will be theirs. They've been away for a couple of days, scattering Rose's ashes near a little cottage she used to stay in to get away sometimes. There's a lake nearby, which she would walk around with Ben and Scamp, and she requested that her ashes be scattered there.

Luke was very fond of Rose. She never had children of her own, and Luke was an only child, so she poured all of her affection onto him. Beth and Luke had been working hard to save up for a house of their own, but now their savings could be spent on redecorating the old home instead.

Luke works in construction with his dad, Tom, and Beth works in a hardware store also owned by Luke's dad. They've only been married a year and, until now, have been living with Luke's parents. They've been together since the summer after they left school. Luke worked with his dad through the summer holidays, and Beth used to hang around at the park near the yard on her lunch breaks. She'd been living alone for months by that point, working two jobs to cover the bills since her parents left. She was getting by, but barely. She was just glad school was over so she didn't have to find jobs that worked around it anymore. Beth and Luke knew each other from school, and Luke had heard all about her parents. She worked at a coffee shop just opposite the yard, and Luke noticed one day that she never seemed to be eating on her lunch break. She would sit on a bench with her head in a book and then go back to work.

One day he packed an extra sandwich and headed over to the park. He sat next to her on the bench, and she fidgeted away a little but looked up at him from her book, smiling shyly. He offered her a sandwich, making a comment about his mother always making him too much food. She took the sandwich, and Luke continued to bring extra for her every day. The conversation started with small talk about their jobs and school and developed over the next few weeks into talk about their families and what they hoped to do in the future. Beth had the feeling that a new part of her life had begun the day Luke sat down next to her and offered her his sandwich. Something about the kindness in his eyes and his genuine smile made her feel safe and comfortable. Beth was conscious that she never had food to bring for their lunch dates, but Luke never made a big deal about it.

One day, while they sat on the wooden park bench, Luke scratched their initials into it with a heart around it. Then he leaned forward, gently brushed a loose strand of hair out of her face, and kissed her softly. Beth felt that fluttering in her stomach that she'd heard people talk about but was sure they must be exaggerating. Luke scratched the date under their initials, and that bench became theirs.

They quickly became inseparable, and Beth felt new hope for the future that she'd never felt before. She finally felt like she had someone to lean on, to help her through life, to love her properly. Luke's parents invited Beth around for dinner every evening, and when his dad learnt about her working two jobs to pay the bills, he offered her a full-time job at his hardware store, paying her enough to make up for the two jobs she had been doing.

Within a year, Beth lived with Luke at his parent's house, leaving her childhood home and all of the bad memories haunting it behind. Beth enjoyed working at the hardware store with the elderly manager, Bill, who had worked there since it had opened. He was almost fifty and needed the extra help since his son, who used to work there with him, left to join the army.

The store was just two streets away from the builder's yard, but work became busy for Luke, and he was away from the yard more often. They still met for lunch when they could, but Beth spent most of her breaks with Bill, which she didn't mind. Sometimes his wife, Angela, would bring in something home-cooked for their lunch, making sure there was enough for Beth too. Angela needed someone to fuss over now that their son had left, and she made the most amazing shepherd's pie.

*

When Beth and Luke finally leave the bed and breakfast and set off, they can't stop smiling. Beth wonders if she should tell him about the possibility of her parents returning in case they randomly turn up, but she decides today isn't the day for that. They've been to Rose's house so many times, but Luke's mother, Jill, said her and Tom would spend a couple of days there tidying up what they could for when they arrive, sorting through Rose's possessions and clearing some storage space for them. Tom's truck is parked outside when they arrive, and Jill walks out of the door carrying some items and loading them into the back of the truck.

When she sees them driving towards her, she waves and smiles brightly.

'Good timing,' she says as they get out of the car. 'We were just finishing up.' She walks over to them and hugs them both tightly. Beth still can't believe how lucky she is—not just to have found Luke, but a new set of parents that treat her like part of their family.

'Come and see what we've done,' she says, taking Beth by

the hand and leading her towards the house. Beth's mouth falls open when they walk into the living room; it's like walking into a different house.

'Wow,' she says. 'It looks so different in here.'

It always seemed quite dark in the living room before, with faded paint on the walls and curtains that were older than Luke, but the curtains have been replaced with new pastel, floral ones, and the walls have been freshly painted. It all looks so bright and inviting now.

'This is amazing,' says Beth as Luke walks in with their bags, looking just as surprised as Beth is. 'It looks so different, doesn't it?'

Jill looks so pleased by their reaction and can't wait to show them more.

'That's not all,' she says. 'Come and see the kitchen. We've painted the cupboards. They were looking a bit old and dreary, but they look like new now. You can replace them one day obviously, but you won't need to rush now.' She leads the way into the kitchen. Beth looks back at Luke, and they smile at each other in disbelief.

'I love it,' says Beth. Nothing she can say feels like enough. 'You've done so much here, I don't know how we're going to repay you.'

Jill waves a hand in the air. 'Don't be silly,' she says. 'There's no need for that. We actually had a great time doing it. Oh, one more thing.' She takes Beth's hand again and leads her upstairs. Luke says he'll follow them up with their bags.

'We've not done a lot up here,' says Jill as they walk into the bedroom, 'but there's new bedding on the bed and some new curtains up in the window. Oh, and we found this painting in the cupboard under the stairs, we thought you might like it, but if not, feel free to get rid.' The painting hangs on the wall opposite their bed, its rich colours and captivating details demanding attention.

'I love that, Eva. Thank you so much.'

Luke enters the room with their bags, noticing the painting first.

'A painting of a family in our bedroom? Are you hinting for grandchildren, mother?'

'Don't be silly, Luke,' says Jill, blushing. 'I just thought it was a nice painting, that's all. Although, you know that would make me happy, but in your own time obviously,' she says, walking out of the room, leaving them alone together in their new bedroom.

'Can you believe this is ours?' says Luke. 'It looks so much better already, doesn't it?'

'It really does. It's quite overwhelming,' she says, trying to fight back tears that rise to the surface unexpectedly, happy tears. Beth wants to enjoy every bit of happiness she can before her parents come back and try to ruin it.

When they go back downstairs, Jill tells them there's a stew on the cooker ready to be warmed up for their dinner. Beth can't believe everything they've done and how happy they are to do it all.

'Honestly, you've been amazing today, you and Tom,' says Beth. 'I can't thank you both enough.'

'Yeah, Mam, thanks for all this,' says Luke, kissing Jill on the cheek. 'I'm just going to pop out to the yard to give Dad a hand loading the truck.'

After they thank them both for the hundredth time, Jill and Tom head home, just a few streets away, leaving Beth and Luke to enjoy their first night in their new home. They fall asleep so quickly that night. It's the most peaceful sleep Beth has ever had.

*

Beth wakes to the sunlight shining through the weave of the

new curtains that Jill put up yesterday, the sun making the colours glow and dance on the walls. She smiles with her eyes still half-closed and reaches over to Luke, but he's not there. She can hear music coming from the kitchen and Luke singing along faintly. She sits up, stretches, and smiles to herself as she gets out of bed and heads downstairs.

'Morning,' she says, walking into the kitchen.

Luke turns around surprised. He didn't hear her coming down.

'Oh hey, I was going to surprise you with breakfast in bed,' he says, standing over the cooker, food sizzling in the pan.

'Sorry, I can go back to bed if you'd like,' she teases.

'Well no, you're here now. Take a seat. I'll bring it over to you.'

She smiles and tiptoes to kiss him on the cheek as she walks past him to the table, the heat from the cooker making her shiver.

'Here you go,' says Luke as he places her cooked breakfast on the table in front of her. 'Breakfast is served.'

'This looks amazing,' she says, trying to talk over the rumbling of her stomach. 'Thank you.'

'Do you want some tomatoes with it?' he asks, heading back over to the cooker for his breakfast.

'Not this morning, thanks,' she replies, her mouth already full of eggs. 'Have you got plans for the weekend?'

'Not much,' he says, shrugging, as he joins her at the table. 'Just hanging around the house with my wife. Actually, I'll have to pick up Ben and Scamp from my mother's later. We could take them for a walk after if you want to?'

'That sounds nice. We should make the most of the good weather,' replies Beth.

A grin starts to spread across Luke's face as he looks at Beth.

'What?' she asks. 'Do I have something on my face?'

'You haven't stopped smiling since you got up this morning. I like seeing you happy like this,' he says, reaching over and taking Beth's hand in his.

'I just can't believe all of this is ours,' she says, gesturing to the house around them. 'It feels like the third chapter of our fairy tale. The first being when we met, and the second our wedding day.'

'I know what you mean,' replies Luke. 'I feel like I could sit here in this room for the rest of my life just looking at you, and I would be just as happy on my last day as I am right now.'

Beth puts her palm gently on Luke's cheek.

'You know you sound like the characters from my romance books sometimes,' she says, and Luke laughs. 'But I think we need to remember that this new start is just that: a start. We've got plenty of time to sit and look at each other and just be happy, but today I want to do what you suggested. You pick up the dogs, who must be missing Rose as much as we are, and then we'll take them for a nice walk. Yes?'

'I guess you're right,' sighs Luke jokingly. 'I'll go get them after breakfast, and you can get dressed ready. Shall we take a picnic?'

'We haven't got any food in yet. We could pick something up on the way though?'

'No need,' says Luke, grinning as he walks over to the kitchen cupboards and opens them. 'My mother stocked these up yesterday and the fridge. I think there's some of everything you would find on a shop shelf.'

Beth laughs in disbelief.

'I am actually speechless,' she says, getting up and looking through the cupboards and fridge full of food. 'She really did think of everything, didn't she?' Luke drapes his arms over her shoulders, and they sway back and forth slowly, not matching the quick tempo of the music playing on the radio, but they're lost in their own little world for a moment.

When Luke leaves to pick up Ben and Scamp, Beth gives the dishes a quick wash and lays them on the draining board before drying them with one of Rose's old tea towels. She holds it to her face when she's finished, hoping for her familiar smell to still be there, but it's been washed away. She makes some sandwiches and takes her time trying to decide what else to pack for their picnic; there's just so much choice. She fills their water bottles, as well as an extra one for the dogs, and packs everything ready to go. She throws in some extra food because no doubt Ben and Scamp will want to share. The two golden retrievers are the loveliest dogs, so large and clumsy and funny. Beth and Luke were surprised when Rose took them in at her age. They were only a year old at the time and full of that relentless puppy energy. They had belonged to a friend of Rose's who passed away and had no other family who could take care of them. They were already used to Rose, and she couldn't bear to see them go to someone who might not take care of them properly. They are three years old now. Beth imagines what they might be like around their future children as she subconsciously touches her stomach. She's two weeks late, but she hasn't told Luke yet. She doesn't want to get his hopes up in case it's a false alarm, although she's never been this late before. She knows she will make a better mother than she had growing up. Her child will never be left alone to fend for themselves.

She heads upstairs to get dressed, choosing a lemon and pink floral cotton dress with buttons down the front. The material dances off her hips like it's being freed from the fitted waistline that imprisons it. She wants to wear it now just in case she won't be able to again for a while. She clips some of her hair back with a few floral hair clips, then grabs a light cardigan in case the weather changes later.

She hears Luke coming through the front door and rushes

downstairs to find Ben and Scamp bouncing excitedly from room to room, trying to take in all the changes, tripping over as they keep changing direction. They stop to greet Beth, then get back to running around.

'You look nice,' says Luke as he kisses her cheek.

'Thank you. I thought I'd dress for the sunshine while it lasts.'

'Shall we take the car down to the country lanes and walk around the fields there? There'll be plenty of room for these two to run around.'

'Sounds good,' she replies. 'I've packed some lunch and some water for the dogs, so I'm ready to go.'

*

Sitting in the middle of a field of bluebells at Beth's request, they unpack their little picnic. Beth made sure to pack extra ham for Ben and Scamp. They've been running around and playing for a while now and are starting to get tired. The smell of food travels through the light breeze, reaching their noses and bringing them leaping over to Beth and Luke. Ben is always the first there when food is around. Scamp just follows along, oblivious to anything except watching what Ben is doing and following suit. They get stuck into the little buffet Beth has laid out for them before lapping up the water and collapsing onto the ground to rest.

Beth and Luke can enjoy their food in peace now.

'When I tidy up Rose's garden out the back, these two will have plenty of space to run around out there,' says Luke.

'And we could get a nice garden bench for us to sit out there with them,' says Beth, smiling. 'Do you think they'll be okay when we're back at work tomorrow?'

'They'll be fine,' replies Luke. 'Mam will pop in around lunchtime to check on them and let them out for a little bit.

Makes me feel grown up all of a sudden, all this responsibility.'

'I know what you mean. I like it though,' says Beth, searching his face for answers to questions she hasn't really asked. 'I think I'm going to collect some bluebells to put in a vase when we get home.'

Ben and Scamp are back on their feet now, following Beth while she picks the flowers. They look like they think they're helping by accompanying her to each patch of flowers and sniffing at them. When she kneels down in a large patch of them, the dogs completely lose focus and jump over her, licking her face. She ends up in a fit of giggles on the ground with two happy dogs jumping over and around her.

This is what Rose must have meant when she said you know when you've met your soulmate because you see new things in them every day that make you smile. Things that have always been there, but you're busy noticing something else for a while. You want to absorb every single thing about them in turn, so that each moment gets the attention it deserves. Each expression, each tone of their voice, or maybe just a moment that you think you needs framing like a photograph. Luke thinks this is one of those moments: Beth laughing with Ben and Scamp draped over her like two fluffy rugs.

When the moment passes and they all catch their breath, Beth suggests they think about making their way back so they can get some rest. A few clouds have moved above them, stealing away the heat and threatening a rain shower.

'It looks like it might rain. Maybe we should pack up,' she says, putting her cardigan on. They pack everything away and head back to the car. As they pull away, a tiredness hits Beth that she hadn't noticed until now.

'I can't wait to have a hot bath, some dinner, and then settle down for the night. I think I need an early night before work tomorrow,' she says.

'I'm kind of tired now too. There's a bottle of wine in the fridge. I know we have to be up for work tomorrow, but one or two glasses won't hurt, will they?' says Luke.

Beth doesn't answer, lost in the scenery flashing by, her thoughts falling out of the window as they go.

'Beth? Fancy some wine tonight?'

'Yeah, maybe,' she says, pulling her eyes away from the window and back to Luke. 'Sorry I was miles away. I was just thinking about Rose. I wish she was still here.'

'Me too. We'll raise a glass to her tonight.'

When they get home, they sit down in front of the TV to rest for a little bit. Beth has put the bluebells she picked in a vase on the kitchen table. Ben and Scamp settle down on their beds for a nap after their busy afternoon.

Luke turns to ask Beth what she wants to watch, but she's already fallen asleep on the sofa. That's not like her; she's usually full of energy. He wonders if she's coming down with something and places a hand softly on her forehead, but there's no sign of a fever. He lays a blanket over her, but she only sleeps for ten minutes before waking up looking confused and still tired.

'Are you okay?' asks Luke. 'You just nodded off.'

'How long have I been sleeping?' she asks groggily, trying to open her eyes properly.

'Not long, maybe like fifteen minutes. Are you feeling okay?'

'I'm fine, I just felt really tired.'

Luke moves over to the sofa and sits next to her, putting his arm around her and letting her rest her head on his shoulder.

'There's some stew left from yesterday. Let me know when you're hungry, and I'll warm it up.'

'Okay, thank you. Maybe we could skip the wine tonight

though?'

'That's okay, we can keep it for Friday after work,' he replies.

Later in the night, Beth falls asleep as soon as her head touches the pillow. Luke wonders if it's maybe just the excitement of moving into their new home that's worn her out. He lays awake for a little while, the streetlight outside illuminating the hypnotic painting of the family on the beach. He feels like there's something hauntingly sad about what should be such a happy picture, but he can't put his finger on what it is. Maybe it's the thought of Beth's childhood and how lonely she must have been growing up with parents like hers. Not even just her parents; it was like literally none of them cared. Some of the neighbours obviously noticed she was left alone often and tried to help when they could. Luke still doesn't understand why no one reported them or said anything to them. She doesn't really like to talk about it much though, so he only really knows the basics and gossip he heard at school.

*

Beth wakes at 7am to the sound of her alarm clock. Luke likes to get up early before their alarm, so he's already up, but Beth likes to soak up every last minute of sleep she can get. She has an appointment with the doctor this morning to do a pregnancy test, but with her late period and the increasing nausea that's getting harder to hide by the day, she already knows the answer.

Her head swirls a little when she sits up, and her stomach does mini cartwheels as she sits at the kitchen table trying to decide whether or not she should have the egg on toast she's craving for breakfast. As much as she loves her job, she already can't wait for work to be over today so she can crawl back into bed.

She plans on telling Luke tonight rather than waiting for the test results. It feels pointless now to keep it to herself when all the signs are there. She feels like she might burst and end up shouting it to the world if she doesn't tell someone soon.

'Morning, baby,' says Luke. 'What do you fancy for breakfast?'

'Morning,' she smiles back at him. 'I think I'll have eggs on toast, but I'll make it this morning. You sit down. What do you fancy?'

'No, it's fine, honestly. I've been up for over an hour. I was getting bored sitting around anyway.'

'Okay,' she says, 'but I'll make dinner later, deal?'

'Okay, deal.'

He walks over to the table, and they shake on it, smiling. Luke kisses Beth on her forehead, then gets to making breakfast. Beth can't wait to tell him later.

'Want a lift to work?' he asks.

'I think I'll walk today. The weather looks good,' she replies, not wanting to tell him just yet about her doctor's appointment.

Bill is already busy when Beth arrives at work after her appointment.

'Good morning, Beth. Is everything okay?' he asks, looking concerned.

'Everything's fine, Bill, thank you. It was just a check-up.'

Beth smiles at the relief on Bill's face.

'Okay, I don't want to lose my favourite worker,' he says.

'I'm your only worker, so I'm not sure that's a compliment, Bill,' says Beth, taking off her jacket and hanging it on the rail.

'You would be my favourite if I had a hundred workers,' he says with his warm smile.

'You're very sweet, Bill. But I'm fine, honestly. What has

Angela delighted us with for lunch today?' she asks, trying to suppress that nausea that's setting in again.

'Salad sandwiches today, and two slices of her Victoria sponge that you love so much,' he replies.

'That sounds perfect,' says Beth, her sickness easing at the thought of her favourite cake.

Their day at the store is fairly busy with regular customers and restocking. The only time they get to sit down all day is when they close for lunch, and, by the end of the shift, Beth is exhausted. She doesn't even realise she's falling asleep waiting for Luke to come and pick her up until the familiar sound of the horn makes her jump awake. She looks around to check Bill hasn't noticed, but he's concentrating on cashing up.

'Bye Bill, see you in the morning,' says Beth as she heads out the front door.

'See you, Beth,' he replies, giving Luke a wave too.

Beth gets in the car, and Luke immediately leans over to give her a kiss.

'How was your day?' he asks, starting the car up and pulling out into the busy town traffic.

'Yeah, it was fine, busy,' replies Beth. 'How was yours?'

'Busy too,' he replies. 'What do you fancy for dinner? Want to pick something up?'

'I fancy chicken. Maybe we could stop at the butchers?

'Okay, let's do that,' he says. 'Lou at work said his wife told him she saw you going into the doctors this morning?'

Beth loves this little town, but word does get around too fast sometimes. She wanted to make this special and tell him later at home, but she doesn't want to lie, and she doesn't think she can keep it any longer. It seems pointless lying for the sake of a few hours and a better location. He parks the car outside the butchers and turns towards her, a mix of concern and anxiousness on his face.

'Are you ill? You've been tired a lot lately,' he says.

'I'm not ill, Luke,' replies Beth, unable to keep the smile off her face. 'I'm pregnant.'

Beth doesn't think she's ever seen someone's facial expression change so quickly. Luke's face lights up with excitement, his eyes brightening and his smile taking up half of his face.

'Are you serious? Are you sure?' he asks.

Beth can't speak; she's so overwhelmed with happiness. She just nods, and Luke practically dives across the car, wrapping his arms around her, making Beth giggle like a child.

'I can't believe it. I'm so happy,' he says into her hair, then pulls away quickly to look at her. 'Are you?'

'Of course, I am,' says Beth, struggling to keep the tears out of her eyes. 'I love you so much, and now we get to start a family of our own, the one we've always wanted.'

'I love you too,' he says, tucking her hair behind her ear. 'This has been the most perfect week. You stay here; I'll go into the butchers. You need to get your rest.'

'I'm not ill, I'm just tired, but at least I know why I'm tired now.'

'Still, I want to take care of you and fuss over you, so make the most of it. And you won't get much rest when the little fella comes along,' he says, and she knows he's imagining it all in his head, like she's been doing.

'It could be girl,' she says.

'My instincts tell me the first one will be a boy.'

'A mini you for you to play football with? That sounds nice.'

'Do you want anything else from here?' asks Luke, gesturing towards the butchers.

'No, I'm good, thank you.'

'Okay, won't be long.'

The smile doesn't leave his face at all as he leans into kiss her again and bounces out of the car into the butchers.

Beth leans her head against the headrest of the car seat and closes her eyes, fully content but still exhausted. The painting from their bedroom pops into her head—the family on the beach, a glimpse of their future maybe. She's always looked forward to making nice memories like that with her own family. She's not sure what it is, but there's something about that painting that makes her feel strange whenever she looks at it. It's a happy painting, but there's something a little odd about it. Sometimes she feels like it's watching them while they sleep.

Luke returns with their food, and Beth manages to make a roast dinner when they're home, with a little help from Luke as her energy drops towards the end. They're both exhausted afterwards, but Luke still hasn't stopped smiling since they were in the car.

When they get to bed that night and say their goodnights, Beth finds herself staring at the painting, illuminated by the glow of the streetlight outside their bedroom window. She thinks about her parents, hoping they'll never show up on her doorstep, and about how good things are with Luke and how good they will be in the future. She knows her parents are due to arrive back in the country soon, so she'll have to tell Luke about it before they turn up unannounced. They'd never call or write first.

Beth falls asleep with Luke's hand gently resting on her stomach. Her last thought before drifting off to sleep is that she wishes her parents were no longer around, that she would never have to think about them or concern herself with what they're doing ever again.

You might think that the news the following morning of the car crash that killed both of her parents in France might still upset her a little, but it doesn't. All she can think about is that she didn't want them near her, Luke, or their child, and now they never will be. She had no love left for them.

As she eats her breakfast at the table, Luke watching her carefully for some kind of reaction to the news, she thinks someone must be looking down on them, maybe Rose. She doesn't tell Luke that she wished her parents would disappear for good. Someone must have been listening, thinks Beth. Now her wish has come true.

Clara

Beth and Luke were the sweetest couple. Ella's story definitely changed something in Clara. She didn't want to see misery and unhappiness anymore; it felt like too much of a burden to carry any longer. She couldn't, however, let Beth's parents come back into the lovely life she had built with Luke and blow it all up, so she did what she had to do. People say one good turn deserves another. A part of Clara still believed that one bad turn also deserves another.

Beth and Luke were living a life so similar to the one Clara had wanted for herself, but Luke was a better man than Jack could have been. The couple continued to enjoy every moment of their lives, filling their home with the sound of little feet and laughter and tears. Clara got to stick around and watch them raise their two sons and daughter.

For the first time in a very, very long time, Clara began to feel something similar to happiness. She wasn't happy in the way that Luke and Beth were, but there was a calmness inside her that she had not felt since she was a young girl. She was content and relaxed, and she wished she could have stayed in their home for the rest of eternity. Unfortunately, time kept moving outside of the painting, and the people who owned it would continue to move on without her too.

When Beth and Luke's children moved out to go to university, they decided to move from their big family home to a smaller apartment. Their home suddenly felt too big when it was just the two of them again. They reluctantly let the painting go to a charity shop with all the other belongings they no longer had space for. Beth secretly hoped it would give someone else as much good luck and happiness as they'd had in their lives. She always felt a special connection with it. Maybe it would help out some other family at the beginning of their story.

By the time Clara reached Sue, the times had changed again. Music continued to change, as did the fashion and trends. Clara enjoyed watching the changes unfold. Sue and Jesse were younger than Beth and Luke, not long out of school and navigating a new world of adulthood and big decisions.

Sue was a passionate songwriter, open and uninhibited. She didn't try to hide her flaws or make herself appear to be something she wasn't. Clara really liked that about her. She had a good sense of humour too, which made living on her bedroom wall quite fun.

As confident as Sue seemed, she was unsure of her future and what steps to take to get to where she wanted to be. Clara was more than happy to help. By this point, she had begun to feel more like her old self before she met Jack. Clara had always been kind and considerate before, and she felt like she had found that part of herself again.

Watching Beth and Luke raise their children had made her think often about her own child, but she kept fighting it and pushing those thoughts away. Her and Jack had discussed having children, just before their wedding day. Jack asked Clara how many children she would like to have, and she had said maybe three or four, but she wanted to get the farm up and running properly first. Jack said he wanted more, but Clara joked that if he wanted more, he would have to divorce her and find another wife.

'Maybe I will,' he had joked, or at least Clara had thought he was joking. They never really mentioned it again, and Jack had no idea about Eliza. Clara was long gone before she ever had a chance to tell him she was expecting.

Sue and Jesse

Sue can't wait to get home after her fourth twelve-hour shift in a row this week, the smell of chemicals lingering on her clothes, hair, and skin. Luckily, the cosmetics factory where she works is only a five-minute walk from her home. She can't wait to jump in the shower, wash the smell off her, and crawl into bed. She pops in the local shop on her way home as usual to get some snacks for later and a packet of cigarettes. She knows she shouldn't smoke, but it relaxes her.

Jesse is standing at the bus stop across the road; he would have known she'd be walking home at this time. Jesse broke up with her a few days ago, and they haven't seen each other since. Sue has avoided walking past his house and the places he usually hangs out with his friends. She thinks he's an arsehole for telling her that he loves her and then breaking up with her out of nowhere. She's only sixteen, and people tell her it's not really love at sixteen. She hates the condescension of that statement; how do they know how she really feels? They always had a laugh together and enjoyed each other's company, no matter what they were doing, even if it was just watching TV together, or listening to music, or playing video games.

Jesse always listened intently when Sue played the songs she wrote for him on her piano and always told her how talented she was.

She can't understand why he broke up with her all of a sudden, with no real reason for it either. She had started learning to play the video games he likes so they could play them together. She wasn't very good at them, but it was fun for her trying to beat him, even though she never did.

Sue remembers their first date. It wasn't really a date, but when you're sixteen, your options are limited. They walked around the village together, holding hands and talking about everything and anything. Sue spent her first kiss wondering if she had cleaned her teeth properly, thinking maybe she should have brought TicTacs. It wasn't exactly the romantic first kiss like the ones she'd seen in films and heard about from her friends, but it was nice when she stopped worrying and relaxed into it. Jesse's a good-looking guy with his wavy, brown, medium-length hair that falls naturally into place. He has deep brown eyes and a smile that's contagious to everyone around him.

Sue's friend, Nicola, says the predictable clichés that everyone's heard over and over: 'There's plenty more fish in the sea', and 'you're better off without him, anyway'. Sue doesn't really want to hear that right now. She wants to wallow in the sadness of it all. Nicola was never very supportive of her relationship with Jesse anyway. Sue doesn't think she would be supportive of any relationship she has because it means they get to hang out less, and, truth be told, Sue has missed spending more time with her friends anyway.

Sue and Jesse grew up in the same village and went to school together, but Jesse didn't ask Sue out until the summer disco, just after they had left school. They had always been close, but always just friends, despite the attraction and obvious flirtation.

Sue decided not to go to college. The only thing that's ever interested her is music. She plays piano and writes her own songs, but she's not totally naïve. She knows that it won't be easy to achieve, so for now, she plans to continue working at the factory to save up some money while writing songs in her spare time. The cosmetics factory isn't exactly glamorous or fun, but the pay is okay for now. She gives her parents some money towards the bills, puts some in her savings, and has enough left for cigarettes and nights out with her friends. When she turns seventeen, she can put some of it towards driving lessons. The twelve-hour shifts drag, and doing four in a row is draining. She wonders if Jesse was sick of her working and not being able to see her as much, or if he got bored of how tired she was after work. Jesse certainly thinks he deserves all the attention in the world. Since they broke up, Sue bounces back and forth between his good points and his bad points. She tries to convince herself that the bad outweighs the good and wonders if she ever really liked him more than a friend anyway. She misses hanging out with him, but is that romantic love or platonic love? She never dreamed of a future together, but she's not sure anyone does at sixteen. She feels like a confused teenager, which she reminds herself is actually what she is, so she doesn't need to figure everything out immediately.

She tries to ignore Jesse standing across the road, but he jogs across and catches up, despite her quickening her pace.

'Hey, squirt,' he says, a mischievous smile on his face.

She sighs loudly. She's really not in the mood for him today.

'You know I hate being called that, Jesse.'

'Sorry, baby,' he says, a playful tone still lingering in his voice.

'Yeah, that too.'

She rolls her eyes and adjusts the strap of her bag on her shoulder, picking up her pace a little again.

'Someone's in a bad mood,' he says, realising that his attempts to keep the mood light are failing.

She stops so quickly that he doesn't realise, taking a few more steps before turning to stop in front of her.

'I am exhausted, and I would like to get home as quickly as possible. Did you want something?' she asks.

'Yes, actually.' He pauses, smiling at her.

She folds her arms and taps her foot impatiently, waiting for him to tell her what it is that he wants.

'Don't you want to know what it is?' he asks.

She gives him a deathly stare, and he surrenders.

'I want my girlfriend back.'

She scoffs and pushes past him, continuing her brisk walk home.

'Yeah, that won't be happening.'

'Why not?' he asks. 'We were good together, weren't we?'

'Yeah, until you dumped me for no reason. We can hang out as friends, I told you that already, but I don't want to be your girlfriend again.'

'Harsh,' he says, his hands sinking into his pockets, the playful tone in his voice gone.

'Yeah, it was harsh when you broke up with me out of nowhere with no explanation.'

'I'm sorry...'

'I don't care,' says Sue, interrupting him.

'Bloody hell. Okay. I was just going to say I'm sorry for being an idiot, and I'm sorry I upset you. But I do miss you, and I would like to hang out if you would like to?'

Sue shrugs and nods in response.

'Will you be a bit less mean when we hang out?'

She tries not to, but the corner of her mouth curls into a slight smile, and he takes that as a sign that she's forgiving him.

'You want to come over tomorrow or are you working?'

'I'm off tomorrow,' she says.

'Do you want to come over for tea? Mam's making a stew and she asked if you would be coming round. We can hang out for a bit after?'

They've almost reached Sue's house, and she's slowed down a little.

'Yeah, fine, what time? Around five?'

'Perfect,' he says, trying not to smile too wide in case it puts her off again.

'Right, well, see you tomorrow then,' she says, pushing

open the garden gate and heading down the path to her front door.

'See you tomorrow,' he calls after her.

*

Sue wakes at 7.30am, the sun creeping through the gaps in her curtains. She collapsed into bed by 10pm last night after feasting on her mother's home-made lasagna, followed by home-made sponge cake, and fell straight to sleep. That was the best sleep she's had in ages, probably because her mother moved that painting from above her bed. She put it there, insisting it would brighten up the room up a bit, but Sue kept getting the weird feeling that it was going to fall on her head while she slept. She kept waking up in the night thinking it was coming at her. Her mother said she was being silly and only moved it to the opposite wall instead, saying there was nowhere else in the house to hang it. Sue said maybe she shouldn't hang it up then, and her mother gave her the same glare she had given Jesse the day before, so she left her to it. Now that it's not hanging above her head though, Sue kind of likes it. The family playing on the beach look so happy together, and the details are quite captivating. Sue finds herself staring at it for ages sometimes without realising.

She thinks back to yesterday and feels like maybe she was too rough on Jesse, but then reminds herself that he did break up with her quite harshly. She wasn't in the mood for him after putting up with her supervisor all day, dancing around the factory floor singing I'm Too Sexy, which he really isn't. Deeply Dippy would be a more appropriate description.

She lazes around in bed for a while, reading through some lyrics she'd been working on a few weeks ago and enjoying not having to rush around getting ready for work. She hears a knock at the door, and then her mother calls up the stairs.

'Jesse's here. Shall I send him up?'

'Yeah, okay,' replies Sue, sitting up in bed and running her hand through her hair, trying to tidy it up a little bit. Jesse pops his head around the door with a sheepish grin on his face.

'I thought I was supposed to be at yours at five?' says Sue, a little more abrupt than she meant to.

'That's what we said, yeah,' he says, dropping down onto the edge of the bed. 'I won't stay long, I'm off to town with my dad soon. I just wanted to check if you're still up for coming over later and to say I'm sorry for yesterday.'

'I'm sorry too. I was just tired after my shift, that's all. I'll be over later, wouldn't miss your mam's stew. Not as nice as my mother's, of course,' she says as her mother pops her head around the door.

'Aye, aye. Do you want a cup of tea, Jesse?'

'No thanks,' he says. 'I'm not stopping, my dad's picking me up now.'

'No problem, love. Sue, do you want one?'

'Yes, please. I'll come down for it now.'

Sue's mother leaves them alone again, and Jesse shuffles on the bed nervously, as though he wants to say something but isn't sure whether he should.

'You are okay with just hanging out as friends, right?' asks Sue.

'Yeah, course I am,' he says a little too quickly. 'I just miss hanging out with you.'

Sue wishes Jesse would act like this all the time, genuine and nice, instead of trying to act cool and not bothered about anything.

'Okay, me too.'

They smile shyly for a second before Jesse gets up off the bed.

'Okay, well, I'll see you later then, yeah?'

'Yeah, see you later.'

Sue intends to get up and go downstairs for her tea, but leans back against the headboard and zones out, staring at the painting opposite. She remembers when her and Jesse went to the beach with all their friends, all of them carrying beach towels and spare clothes in their backpacks, taking up the backseats of the bus, splashing about in the water, and sunbathing on their towels. The boys dug a big hole and flicked the sand at the girls as they tried to lay peacefully in the sun. Later on, Jesse had bought Sue an ice cream cone, and they sat holding hands away from the group as the sun set behind the town, casting a golden pink glow over everything.

Sue's mother walks in with her tea, pulling her out of her thoughts.

'Sorry, I was going to come down for it,' she says.

'That's alright. I thought you might still be tired, so I brought it up for you to have in bed. I'll make you some breakfast when you're ready to come down.'

'Thanks, Mam.'

Sue knows she'll have to get up soon so she doesn't end up wasting her day off. Days off are for piano practise and songwriting. She taught herself to play the piano and to read music when she was a kid. Her love for playing started with her Bontempi keyboard that her parents bought her for Christmas when she was six years old. She loved it and would spend hours playing on it every day. She still has it in the corner of her bedroom; she doesn't think she'll ever be able to part with it.

After her tea, Sue heads downstairs for breakfast, then gets dressed and sits at her piano. She doesn't get as much time to play anymore with work. She's been struggling the last week or so with writing songs, though. The lyrics don't seem to be coming to her as easily as they usually do and she doesn't know why. After a while of trying and failing to come up with anything new and interesting, she practises some songs that she's been learning to play instead, adding in a few of her favourites too.

The day flies by, and, before she knows it, it's time to get ready to go to Jesse's. It always amazes her how hours at the piano can feel like ten minutes. She changes out of her comfy loungewear into a pair of light blue denim bootcut jeans and a fitted t-shirt. After applying a bit of foundation and mascara, the only make-up she really wears, she heads out the front door and makes her way to Jesse's house, looking forward to spending some time with him.

*

Jesse's mother, Pam, opens the door after Sue's first knock, swirling food around in her mouth and trying to blow a bit too late.

'That'll teach me not to blow, won't it?' she says, holding a hand up in front of her mouth. 'Come in, love. Jesse's in his room, you can go straight up if you like.'

Sue walks in after Pam, closing the door behind her.

'You're staying for tea, are you?' she asks Sue.

The smell of stew wafts in from the kitchen, and Sue's stomach does a quiet rumble.

'Yes please, Pam.'

Sue heads up the stairs and finds Jesse sitting on his bed with his headphones on. Sue can hear the music from the doorway. He doesn't notice her there, lost in whatever he's listening to, so she stands and watches him for a moment. He looks more grown up when he's deep in thought like this. After a minute or so, he looks up at her and jumps a little.

'Hey, are you stalking me?' he asks jokingly, taking off his headphones. 'Why didn't you call me?'

'I didn't want to disturb you. You looked miles away.'

She sits on the edge of the bed next to him.

'What are you listening to?' she asks.

He puts the headphones over her ears and plays the end of the song. It's a song she's never heard, but it's completely different from any of the music Jesse has listened to before.

'It's good, I like it,' she says, smiling, handing the headphones back to him.

'How's your writing going?' he asks.

'Not great. I couldn't write anything today.'

'How come? You always seem to find it so easy.'

'Not always,' she says, shaking her head slightly.

'Well you had such a lovely way with words yesterday when you were in a mood,' he says teasingly. 'I think you'll make a great songwriter.'

She rolls her eyes at his little dig.

'It's not always just about the words; it's about the meaning behind them. Sometimes it's just about the words, though. Like when I called you an idiot, I just meant you're an idiot.'

Jesse grabs a pillow from behind him and throws it at Sue playfully. She picks it up and throws it back, then moves to sit next to him with her feet up on the bed.

Jesse turns to look at Sue, and his face has changed from playful to serious.

'What's wrong?' asks Sue.

He opens his mouth, hesitates, then looks away from her as he starts speaking in a low voice.

'I'm going away for a bit. My dad's got a mate up in Bristol who needs help with a big gardening project. Dad's got too many jobs on at the minute, so he asked if I'd like to go instead. I've done a bit before, so I know enough to get started, and everything else I'll learn as I go. I quite like the idea of working outdoors. The job pays really well, and it lasts for about three months. I can carry on working for my dad when I get back then.'

His speech gets quicker as he goes on, like he doesn't want to give Sue a chance to react in case she takes it badly. Her eyes are glazed over as she stares at nothing in particular, trying to process how she feels about Jesse leaving for three months. After a minute, she clears her throat.

'When are you leaving?' she asks. Her thoughts are bouncing around so quickly in her head that she can't finish one before the next one comes along. She said she didn't want to get back together with Jesse, but she had kind of thought it might happen over time if they kept hanging out as friends. She hadn't expected that he wouldn't be around at all. She doesn't want him to go, but she knows it would be unfair to ask him to stay.

'I'm not sure exactly, but it'll be this week some time.'

'Wow, that's soon,' she says, her stomach doing flips. 'I don't know what to say.'

'I could ring and text you every day, if you want? I know you said you didn't want to get back together, but you know I feel the opposite. Maybe we could just keep talking while I'm away and see how things go until I get back?'

'Yeah, maybe,' she says, not really paying attention as her mind is racing.

'Are you okay, Sue?' he asks, taking her hand in his, his eyebrows furrowed slightly with concern. 'If you don't want me to go, I could probably get out of it. I'm sure it would be fine.'

'No, don't do that,' she says quickly, looking at him finally. 'You should go if you want to go. I'm fine. Just a bit of a shock, that's all.' She tries to sound convincing, but her voice trembles slightly, and her eyes begin to fill with tears, no matter how hard she tries to keep them away. Jesse quickly puts his arm around her.

'I'm sorry, Sue,' he says. 'I really didn't think you'd mind at the moment.'

She wipes at her eyes before any tears can escape and shakes her head.

'I'm just being silly,' she says. 'I'm happy for you, really. It sounds like a good opportunity for you, and it's only three months. It's not that long, really, is it? And we can do like you said. We can talk every day and see how things go until you get back.'

She knew she wouldn't be able to keep her distance from him for long, no matter how much she's insisted she doesn't want to be his girlfriend anymore. She realises now how much she enjoys having him in her life and how strong her feelings for him really are. He's been her best friend as well as her boyfriend for so long. She desperately wants to tell him to stay, but she knows she can't. She probably wouldn't be able to get the words out anyway. She can barely take a breath.

She tries to pull herself together, taking a deep breath and sitting up straight.

'I'm glad we made up before you have to leave,' she says, smiling as convincingly as she can manage.

They spend the rest of the evening playing video games, not talking anymore about him leaving. For the next couple of hours, they talk and laugh like it's any other evening they spend together. Even when Jesse walks Sue home, they still don't talk about it.

Jesse holds Sue's hand the whole way back, and it's like they're the only two people to exist in the whole village. Sue realises it's the little things like this that she will miss the most when Jesse is away.

*

Sue lies awake in bed, unable to switch off her mind. She tries to think about it logically, trying to leave her emotions out of it. Bristol isn't really that far. She could always go to visit Jesse sometimes when she's not working. Plus, she realises, he'll probably be back every now and then to visit his parents too. They're a very close family; it's unlikely that he'd go there for three months without coming back to visit sometimes. They can discuss all of this tomorrow, but Sue already feels better with these thoughts in mind. She finally settles into a deep sleep, woken up not much later by a noise at her window. She switches on the lamp next to her bed, trying to focus her sleepy eyes, and almost chokes on her own breath when she sees a face at the window. The face smiles at her, and she realises it's Jesse. Sue rushes out of bed and opens the window.

'What the hell are you doing, you idiot? You nearly gave me a heart attack,' she says in a loud whisper, trying not to wake her parents.

'Come with me,' says Jesse breathlessly, like he'd just run all the way over here.

'Come with you, where?' says Sue, still half asleep. He rolls his eyes at her.

'Bristol, obviously.'

'Oh,' she says, surprised. She trips over her words, not knowing how to respond. She tries to say it kinder, but all she can get out is, 'I can't.'

His face falls. 'Why not?'

'I have a job, and my parents are here. I can't just leave for three months. I'll have no job to come back to.'

'We can figure all that out. You can find a temporary job there. Maybe my dad could put in a word for you somewhere? Please, Sue. I don't want to leave without you.'

He looks so sincere and so sad at the thought of leaving without her that she just wants to say yes and pack up her stuff and go with him right now, but she's trying to be sensible.

'I don't know,' she says.

'Will you think about it at least?'

She's already thinking about it—her and Jesse living together, coming back to each other after a long day of work, discovering a new place, and meeting new people together. He looks so desperately hopeful, so she agrees that she'll think about it.

'But that doesn't mean I will change my mind,' she says, not wanting to give false hope. 'I'll just sleep on it.'

'Okay,' he says, a tone of disappointment in his voice. Sue can't stop a little smile breaking onto her face, knowing that Jesse hates the thought of leaving without her so much, but she turns her face away to hide it.

'We'll talk tomorrow then, yeah?' he asks.

'Okay,' she says, and they say goodnight.

Sue closes her curtains and, in the corner of her eye, notices that the painting on the wall is slanted, so she walks over to straighten it up. She gets back into bed and pulls the covers right up over her, realising how cold she'd gotten from standing by the window. She looks at the painting again, remembering that she had been looking at it as she drifted off to sleep, and it had been straight then. She assumes she'll be awake for hours, contemplating Jesse's proposal to go to Bristol with him, but instead she drifts off to sleep surprisingly quickly, thinking about a painting that she's pretty sure moved on its own.

*

Sue wakes with an odd sense of relief and optimism. She knows what her decision is, and she feels like she's doing the right thing. As sad as she is that he's leaving, Sue's decided not to go to Bristol with Jesse. As much as she wants to, she doesn't want to live her life around what someone else wants to do. She's too young to give him that kind of commitment. She wants to keep her job, continue to save money, and keep working on her songwriting. She's still upset about Jesse leaving, and she knows she'll miss him, but she can see it from a clearer perspective now. Three months isn't really that long. They'll still talk all the time, and they'll have plenty of time together when he's back.

Sue's mother taps on the bedroom door and pops her head in.

'Was that Jesse I heard last night?' she asks.

'Mam, you must have got ears like a bat.'

'I do. I hear everything; you remember that. What was he doing, knocking at the window like a little Romeo in the middle of the night then?' She sits on the edge of the bed, ready for all the details.

'He wants me to go to Bristol with him, but I'm not going to,' she says decidedly.

'Why's that?' she asks. 'Not that I want you to go. I'd rather you didn't, to be honest, but I would have thought you'd want to go. You two have been inseparable for years.'

'I've got my job and writing to do. It's not the right time for me to go swanning off like that,' says Sue, and her mother looks proud.

'Good for you,' she says. 'You do what you want to do. Don't go chasing some bloke around and forgetting yourself.'

'Some bloke?' says Sue laughing. Her mother tuts.

'You know what I mean. You know I like Jesse, but you're both so young. You've got plenty of time for a relationship later on.'

'Yeah, I know,' says Sue, thinking about how she's going to tell Jesse all this later on. 'Do you want to be me today and go tell him that?'

'Do you want to be me and do all the housework today?

Starting with washing your dad's underwear?'

'Mam, that's gross. I'll just go tell Jesse myself,' says Sue, throwing off her quilt and getting out of bed.

'Are you going to tell him now?'

'I'm just going to get dressed. He said he'd come over here but didn't say what time.'

Sue puts her dressing gown on and barely gets to the top of the stairs when someone knocks at the front door.

'I'll get it,' she yells to her mother.

She rushes down, not caring that her hair is a mess or that she hasn't brushed her teeth yet. She swings open the door and lets the words fall out of her mouth a little too quickly.

'I'm not coming. I'm sorry,' she says.

'Wow, okay. Straight to the heart, didn't even see the knife coming,' says Jesse, holding a hand to his heart and wincing jokingly. 'Can I come in now?'

'Sorry,' says Sue, blushing a little and stepping out of the way for him to come inside. 'Do you want to head up to my room?'

Jesse leads the way, and they both perch themselves on the edge of her bed.

'I didn't mean to blurt it out like that, sorry,' says Sue. 'I just didn't want you to get your hopes up, that's all.'

'Well, mission accomplished,' he says, trying to laugh it off a little, but he can't hide the disappointment from his face.

'I know I don't have a filter sometimes,' she says, feeling guilty for the way she told him so abruptly.

'Sometimes? Now you're being too easy on yourself.'

'I'm sorry,' she says again, and he nods, not looking at her. She leans in a little closer, and he turns, their foreheads pressed together, eyes closed, her hand gently resting on the top of his back.

'Have you packed?'

'I have.' He smiles softly at her, brushing some loose

strands of hair out of her face, his fingers lingering on her cheek. 'I am dreading leaving without you now.'

'We can do like you said,' says Sue reassuringly. 'We can talk on the phone every day, and maybe I could even come and visit you when we both have a day off? I could come up for the day or something.'

'That would be cool,' he says, smiling and relaxing a little. 'I'll be back every two weeks anyway, even if it's just for the day. Probably on weekends, so try to keep your calendar open for me, okay?'

They hug for a second, but they both feel the tears coming and pull away, trying to hide them from each other.

'I'll be here,' she says. 'You know that.'

He nods and clears his throat. He wants to change the subject and enjoy their time together before he goes.

'Written any songs lately?'

'I think I've got a couple new ones that I haven't shown you yet. I wrote the lyrics down in a separate notebook so you can read them while you're away if you want?'

His face brightens knowing that she was thinking of him.

'Yeah, course I will, thanks. I'll be back next weekend for the day so you can come over if you want? I'll have to spend some time with my mam and dad as well.'

'Yeah, I'll come over in the afternoon, shall I? You can spend some time with them first then.'

'Sounds good,' he says, his disappointment about her not going with him seeming to fade now that there are plans in place. 'A week's not that long, is it? I've got about an hour before I have to get home and get ready to leave. Are you gonna pop over to say goodbye?'

'I'd rather not, if you don't mind,' she says. 'You know I hate goodbyes. If you've got an hour, do you want some breakfast before you go? I'm sure my mother wouldn't mind making you some too.'

'Yeah, okay, if she doesn't mind. I haven't eaten anything yet this morning.'

Sue goes downstairs to ask her mother if she could make Jesse some breakfast too, then nips into the bathroom to brush her teeth and hair and get dressed quickly. Her naturally straight hair has also been the envy of her friends. Just a quick brush and it all falls neatly into place just above her shoulders. She pops her head back into her bedroom.

'Sorry, I had to get changed. Mam's making breakfast. Do you want to come down?'

'Yeah, okay. I was just thinking I should have brought my games console over for you. You could use the practice while I'm away.'

'Don't kid yourself, I let you win half the time.'

'Yeah, right,' he says, laughing as he follows her down to the kitchen.

'I hear you tried to steal our daughter away with you, Jesse,' says Sue's mother as they sit at the kitchen table. Jesse blushes and stutters over his reply.

'Mam,' says Sue, glaring at her.

'What? I'm just kidding,' she says.

'Sorry about that,' says Jesse. 'Didn't wake you, did I?'

'No, I was still awake,' she replies, dishing out their breakfast and putting their plates on the table. 'Just heard the ladder going up against the wall.'

'And you didn't think it could've been someone coming to murder me in my sleep?' says Sue. 'Thanks, Mam.'

'I figured if it wasn't Jesse, you'd probably scream or something,' she says, winking at Jesse.

'Maybe I wouldn't have been able to. Did you think of that?'

'No, sorry, love,' her mother replies casually.

'Do you hear this?' Sue says to Jesse. 'I'll probably be murdered in my sleep while you're away.'

'Oh, stop being dramatic, Sue,' her mother says, laughing.

'I'm still failing to see the funny side, Mam,' says Sue, but she's smiling, and her mother knows she's only joking.

When Jesse leaves, they decide not to make a big deal of it. They remind themselves they'll see each other in just over a week, so they just kiss and hug, lingering a little longer than normal but without dragging it out.

*

The first week flies by quicker than Sue had expected. She spent most of the week working, writing and over Nicola's house. Nicola isn't interested in hearing about Jesse, as usual, which Sue resents a little but it is nice to have the distractions to make the time go quicker.

It's been a good week for her song writing. Now that things have settled with her and Jesse, she's found it easier to concentrate on it again. She decided to treat herself towards the end of the week with a trip to town to buy herself some new clothes. Summer is approaching so she got herself a couple of dresses to go with the warmer weather.

She's looking forward to seeing Jesse this weekend. They've been speaking every day, and last time they spoke he told her he has a surprise for her when he's home. She wishes he hadn't mentioned it though, as she's been desperate to know what the surprise is and can't stop her mind from wondering and hoping that he might be home sooner than he thought.

If this week has taught her anything though, it's that even though she's missing Jesse, she can be productive and happy in her own company. She knows they'll get through these three months just fine.

When Saturday arrives, she's like a child waiting to go to a birthday party, checking the time all day until it's time to leave for Jesse's. She wears one of her new dresses, a simple shift style dress that sits just above her knees. The fabric is soft and flowing and sprinkled with different coloured flowers. She also wears her new earrings and necklace. While getting ready, she notices her painting is at an angle on the wall again. For a split second, she has the crazy idea that it always happens when she's thinking about Jesse. It happened when he turned up at her window and when they got off the phone a few nights ago, and now again while she's getting ready to go and see him, the surprise he has for her fluttering around in her mind. She straightens it once again, pausing for a moment to make sure it stays in place.

'Are you trying to tell me something?' she asks, then laughs at herself for talking to a painting and looks around to check nobody witnessed it.

She almost breaks into a run as she gets near Jesse's house. He's already standing at the front door waiting and walks towards her when he sees her. He lifts her up in a spin, and she laughs at the cheesiness of it, like something from a romcom. Sue's not usually one for soppy moments or public displays of affection, but she enjoys it.

'You look amazing,' says Jesse as he wraps her up in a big hug. 'I've missed you so much.'

'Me too,' she says, taking in the smell of him and the way his arms feel around her.

'Good, maybe my news later will be good news then,' he says, pulling away from her and smiling cheekily.

'You're not sure it will be?' she asks.

'Not really yet, but I'm hoping it will.'

He takes her hands and leads her towards the house, but she stops.

'Just tell me, please,' she says.

'Can we at least get in the house first?' he says. 'I'll make us some drinks, and then I'll tell you. Then we can go for a walk or pop into town for some food, maybe?'

'Okay,' she says reluctantly and continues walking to his house.

She sprints upstairs after saying hi to Jesse's parents, as if her rushing will make him move quicker. She sits on his bed while he gets their drinks and puts her feet up, unable to stop fidgeting while she waits for him to come up. The window is open, letting in a slightly warm breeze. She feels like she's not been in this room for ages, even though it's only been just over a week. Jesse brings up some lemonade with ice and puts them on his bedside table.

He hasn't even sat down yet, but Sue is impatient and feels like she's waited long enough.

'Go on then, spill. What's the surprise?'

'Okay,' he says, taking a breath and sitting on the bed next to her. 'So I know you said you didn't want to come to Bristol, but...'

'We've already talked about this,' she interrupts. 'I don't want to leave my job, and I...'

'Let me finish?' he says softly, and she apologises and motions for him to continue.

'The guy I work for, his mate runs a bar, and he's looking for more staff. It's not just a bar though, it's a music venue. They do open mic nights every week for new songwriters, and sometimes they have important people from the music industry there. I hope you don't mind, but I told him about you and showed him the lyrics you wrote down for me, and he said he'd be happy to give you a job, and you would know when there's important people in so you could play at the open mic nights too. They'd train you up to work in the bar, you don't need experience, and you could get your music out there.' He's getting more and more excited as he goes on, feeling like there's no way she could turn this down. 'So what do you think?'

'Wow,' says Sue, sitting forward and crossing her legs. 'I don't know what to say.'

'But you're interested?' he says hopefully.

'I mean, yeah, of course I am, but that's a really big move.'

'I know it's a lot and it's overwhelming, but you don't have to decide right now. You can think about it.'

'Okay. My mother will be upset if I go, I think.'

'I'm sure she'll be fine. It's not forever, and she'll be able to see that it's a good opportunity for you. You can come home with me on weekends, and it'll be more fun to travel together.'

Sue tries to fight against the idea, but she can't help feeling excited about it all. She doesn't see how she can turn it down this time.

'It's a bit scary,' she says.

'What? Nothing scares you.'

Sue stops for a second, thinking about why she wasn't scared that the painting in her bedroom seems to be moving on its own regularly. She keeps getting the feeling that it's trying to tell her something, but then brushes the idea aside. A painting can't be trying to tell her anything, it's a painting.

'Earth to Sue,' says Jesse, waving his hand in front of her face.

'Sorry, I was thinking,' she says, shaking herself out of her thoughts. 'What if we go up there together and things don't work out with us? Then I'd be alone there.'

'That won't happen,' he says shaking his head. 'Even if we did break up, I would still be your friend. You would never be alone there.'

She can tell that Jesse means what he says.

'That helps,' she says quietly.

'So, you'll come?'

She pauses and takes a deep breath, then nods.

'I don't see how I could turn that down really,' she says

smiling.

He jumps forward and wraps his arms around her, both of them falling back into the headboard and laughing.

'You can come with me to tell my parents though,' she says.

'You just want to watch your mother murder me, don't you?'

'That would be quite funny,' she says, picturing her mother chasing Jesse down the street with a frying pan. She can't help but laugh to herself.

'Okay, stop enjoying that thought so much,' he says.

As they hold hands and chat away on the bed, Sue's stomach flutters with excitement about this new life ahead of her.

Clara

Both Sue and Jesse stayed in Bristol and eventually got their own flat together, both succeeding in what they wanted to do. Jesse got his gardening business going and Sue was singing at different venues as well as writing songs for other well-established singers. Sue's doubts about whether it had been the right move quickly evaporated. Later, when they had two young children running around, Sue's parents moved closer to them which made Sue so happy. They brought the painting from her bedroom with them. Sue hung it in the living room and it remained straight for the rest of its time there.

Clara wanted to give Sue a sign that she should leave with Jesse. She knew it would be best for her, but Sue was such a headstrong, busy person that Clara found it harder to get inside her head. She wasn't sure moving the painting would work, but it did. She used the same move when Sue's mother was trying to decide whether they should move closer to Sue, but Clara thought maybe she couldn't take full credit for that one. She didn't need much convincing to move closer to her daughter.

Clara found herself getting more and more attached to the people she lived with. The old Clara felt long gone, like a different person. The rage and the need for revenge was almost completely gone. The only time she felt it all coming back, was when someone she cared for was in danger.

Watching these people for so long made her ache sometimes for her old life, before it fell apart. Watching the family plan and prepare for Sue's and Jesse's wedding brought back memories of her own wedding day. She remembered being so nervous that morning, nervous but excited. She had nausea from the minute she woke up, her stomach dancing while she got ready. Her mother tried her best to distract her. When she was in her dress and her hair and make-up had been done, Clara's mother walked her over to the full-length mirror, proud tears in her eyes. The wedding dress was sleeveless with a heart-shaped neckline and sequins glimmering at the top. It spread out onto the ground with a delicate layer of lace over the top of the skirt. Her veil had white roses around the top, and her make-up was subtle. She was the most beautiful bride; Jack couldn't take his eyes off her through the ceremony. The flashbacks made Clara smile as she remembered how she felt on that day. Maybe if she had allowed these memories in sooner instead of just looking at the bad, she could have healed and moved on. She thought that if she let them in, they would only add to her sadness, but it felt good to remember that it hadn't all been for nothing, that she was in love and felt loved and had been happy for a while.

After Sue and Jesse, Clara belonged to Lizzy and it was with Lizzy that Clara had her first encounter with an actual ghost, and David was no ordinary ghost.

Lizzy

Lizzy finishes unpacking and takes a look around her new home. She's not seen David, the ghost who came with the house, since she moved in a few days ago. She wonders if he's given up and left now that someone else has moved into his old home, but she has a feeling he'll be back at some point. For some reason, she's not a bit spooked by him. He's seemed so calm each time she's seen him, just sitting in his old armchair, watching quietly. She thinks he's harmless, or she hopes he is. She first saw him when she viewed the house, after a group of teenagers outside shouted at her to 'Watch out for the ghost in the window' before laughing and walking away when she asked what they meant. The estate agent rolled her eyes and tutted at their silliness, but there he was when Lizzy walked into the living room. She didn't give any indication that she could see him sitting there. She thought he had a sad but kind face.

Even though she's not too bothered by his presence, she's hoping to see him again soon so they can have a word about boundaries. She doesn't want him watching her while she sleeps or takes a shower or anything creepy like that. She has a feeling he's not that kind of guy anyway, and she hopes she's right. If not, she may have just made a huge mistake moving in here.

David's old armchair still sits in the corner of the living room, deserted at the moment. Lizzy can't seem to get rid of it; she's not sure why. It seems disrespectful to get rid of it when he's still using it, and she doesn't mind it anyway. The black leather recliner looks like it's seen better days, but Lizzy has filled the house with second-hand furniture anyway, so it fits right in. Most of the furniture has been bought from charity shops. Lizzy doesn't really see the point in buying new when you can get such good deals elsewhere for furniture that's still got plenty of life left in it. She picked up a few finishing touches from the charity shops too, being a sucker for antiques. She found a lovely old jewellery box and a painting of a family playing on a beach that she's hung up in the living room. It brightens the place up a bit. It caught her eye because she thought it was something her grandmother would have liked.

Lizzy lived in Swansea while she was attending uni, but moved back in with her parents after she graduated a couple of years ago. Her parents live in the countryside and Lizzy began to deeply miss the convenience of living in the city, where takeaways can be ordered at all times, there are multitudes of coffee shops to work in when she gets sick of working at home, and there are endless scenic walking routes. After living with her parents for two years and working consistently to increase her savings, Lizzy was more then ready to get her own home. She's queried if the owner of her new house would ever consider selling, but there are no plans for that just yet. At least it wasn't a definite no, though.

Lizzy's grandmother left her some money last year when she passed away. That, along with the money she's saved herself, is enough for her to buy a house and have some left to be comfortable for quite some time. She currently works from home as a freelance accountant. She worked for an accounting company when she left uni but was always eager to be her own boss. After working there for almost two years, she felt she had gained enough experience to set up on her own. She only has three regular clients at the moment but it's a start. She doesn't mind her job, she likes the flexibility of it, and it pays well, but her real ambition is to be a thriller author. She's not sure why, but she already thought that this house would be the perfect setting to work on her first novel before she even viewed it and first encountered David.

Lizzy's mother, Annie, has been trying to help as much as

possible making the house feel like a home. She's already been stocking up the freezer and food cupboards, even though Lizzy insisted there was no need. She has to remind herself that her mother is just trying to take care of her daughter, not insinuating that Lizzy doesn't know how or isn't capable of doing these things herself. She does appreciate everything her parents do for her and has always been close with them both. Her dad, Ron, works at the steel works nearby, and Annie has recently retired from her career as a nursery teacher. She deserves a rest, if only she would. She's always finding ways to keep herself busy, usually by doing things for other people. Lizzy managed to convince her to take up a hobby to keep herself busy, so now she's a keen gardener with a beautiful garden that she insisted on working on all by herself of course.

Lizzy takes a seat on the sage green velour stool by the living room window and looks out on the terraced street. She becomes hypnotised by the rain which is light but intrusive enough to soak you if you were to step outside in it. She's been trying to take notice of her neighbours, trying to work out who she could make friends with on her street. There's an elderly man, Jerry, living opposite her. He's in his seventies and she's seen him a few times out walking his large golden retriever.

Right next door to her is a woman who looks about the same age as Lizzy, but she's only seen her briefly going in and out of the house. She didn't look very friendly or approachable; Lizzy's never seen her talking to anyone else on the street. She was wearing a fancy suit and heels that gave Lizzy vertigo just by looking at them even though she was already quite tall. She has long red, wavy hair and a pale complexion. Lizzy thought she was very pretty but her stern look wasn't doing her any favours.

As darkness descends outside, Lizzy feels an aching in her

muscles and her eyes start to burn with the exhaustion of moving. She changes into a warm pair of pyjamas and snuggles under the duvet, ready for some much-needed sleep. It doesn't take her long to drift off, but she faintly remembers a presence above her before she falls into a deep sleep.

*

David has given Lizzy some space for a couple of days while she moves in and gets settled, but he can't help himself tonight. He quietly sneaks into her bedroom, which already looks so different now that his belongings have been replaced with hers, and watches her drift off to sleep. He knows that this is probably over-stepping but tells himself he won't make a habit of it. He never gets tired anymore, but he misses the tranquillity of sleeping, of shutting everything out for a few hours every night.

Lizzy's now all covered-up under the duvet, laying on her side, her wavy blonde hair cradling her face while she sleeps. She has a friendly way about her, David thinks, and a welcoming smile that he's guessing she wears often. The kind that makes you feel good to be around, at ease. He could stand here all night just watching her, but he knows that would be wrong and he doesn't want to scare her if she were to wake up, so he leaves the bedroom and heads downstairs to the living room instead.

David takes a quick look out the window, the teenagers hanging around outside give him a wave. He doesn't know why some people can see him and some can't. He wishes they couldn't see him though. He pulls the curtains closed again and sits in his comfortable old armchair. He's glad Lizzy seems to want to keep this for now.

He thinks about how settled he was here, how much he

loved having his own place. He was never really one for partying, but his friends were the same, and would often come over to watch the football and rugby or play video games. They'd order a takeaway and have a few quiet beers.

Romance never seemed to be on the cards for him. He had dated but there had never been anyone serious. He wasn't sure why, but he could never get past the dating stage to the more serious relationship stage. Now he never will.

He wonders if Lizzy has a partner, though he hasn't seen anyone or heard any mention of it, and what she's like to hang out with if it turns out she can see or speak to him. He thinks she can but he's not completely sure yet. He thought she looked straight at him when she viewed the house, but it was a very brief glance, barely for a second.

He couldn't help but notice how blue Lizzy's eyes were, the colour of a clear summer sky. He could imagine losing his train of thought easily while looking into those eyes. She seems very confident in herself but he can't tell how honest that is. Sometimes people can just put it on, like a show, to protect themselves. He'll find out soon enough though. He's not sure yet how he should approach her. He wants her to make first contact, but he still doesn't really know if she can see him, and if she can, maybe she would wait for him to say something first.

The truth is, he was hoping Lizzy would move in since her first viewing of the house. He overheard her saying she wanted to be an author and that she was planning on writing a book here. He wants her to write his story, to find out what really happened to him and put it out in the world. He has his suspicions, but he hasn't been able to tell anyone about them. It was always the wrong people who seemed to be able to see him. Until now, that is. He's been writing things down to make sure he doesn't forget any details. He's not sure if his memory will begin to fade over time, or even how long he'll be able to hang around here for.

He made more notes at the library yesterday, just the main details for Lizzy to look over and help her get to know who he was just before he was murdered.

He had only been living here for about a year before it happened. He kept to himself mostly, but he was polite. He would always say hello to the neighbours and frequented a few of the local cafes, but he never really got to know anyone that well. Jerry across the road was the friendliest neighbour, along with his dog, Frank. He worked from home helping businesses with their websites and social media content. It wasn't exactly his dream job but it paid well. Truth be told, he was interested in becoming a writer himself.

His parents and sister live close by, and they visited each other often. His father, Gary, runs his own construction business, and his mother, Christine, is a nurse. Kathy, his sister, is a few years younger than him. They got along well, and David was very protective of her, still is. As you can imagine, it hit the family hard when David died. That was the hardest part for him, seeing how it affected the ones he left behind. He had to stop going to their home. It was too hard for him to see them so upset and not be able to reach out or offer any comfort to them. Maybe when they've had more time to grieve, he'll try to visit them again.

David has written most of this down for Lizzy; he doesn't really want to have to talk about his family too much. It's too hard for him. He doesn't think he'd be able to get through it without breaking down.

He stands in front of the painting Lizzy bought, looking closely at it. It unsettles him, makes him feel as though he's being watched. Ironically, he doesn't like being watched himself.

There's movement upstairs. He hadn't even noticed the light starting to creep through the small gap in the curtains.

He makes himself scarce while Lizzy wakes up and plans to come back later.

*

Lizzy places her coffee cup on the second-hand oak coffee table and makes her way over to the window to open the curtains. The light pours into the room, the sky clear after a miserable day yesterday. She's hoping it stays that way so she can head out for a walk later. She knows the area a little from when she used to pass through sometimes during her uni days. Her street comes off a main road that has a few shops and small businesses along it, with a park at the end that has great views of the city.

She sits down and switches the TV on to watch Good Morning Britain. She likes to keep up with the daily news while she has a coffee.

She knows David has been here because she remembers closing the curtains properly last night, making sure there were no little gaps, but this morning they were slightly apart in the middle, just a small gap but enough to let a streak of light in. She finds herself hoping he'll be back again soon, thinking it would be nice to have a bit of company, as strange as that sounds. At least she can tell him to leave when she wants him to, or she's hoping that'll be the case anyway. He seems to have backed off a little while she's been moving in, which could be a good sign that he'll respect her boundaries and her privacy. Unless she's wrong and he's biding his time to jump out and give her the scare of her life any second now. She's certainly got the imagination of a writer, constantly making up scenarios that she doesn't really want to consider a possibility.

She considers having a shower soon to warm up. Despite the clear skies and the sun shining through the window, it's still quite cold here this morning, and she's yet to figure out how exactly the heating system works.

When she's showered and dressed, she tries to decide between taking a walk in the park and making the most of the dry weather or going to a coffee shop and maybe getting to know some of the locals. She knows she won't have time to do both today, as her parents will be around later. They're picking up the cat she's adopted from a cat rescue place about an hour away. She's only a year old, and her previous owner couldn't take care of her anymore. Lizzy has been to visit her twice; she's a beautiful tabby named Tilly who seemed to lap up Lizzy's love and attention. Lizzy made a joke about being twenty-four years old and already living alone with a cat, but it suits her just fine. Her parents will be dropping her off around lunch time.

The weather is hard to read around this time of year as summer ticks over into autumn, but it is Wales, so the weather is unpredictable all year round anyway. Lizzy always struggles to know how to dress when it's like this, starting off chilly in the morning but often back to the summer heat by afternoon. It's dry so far today so she's going to risk it and just go with a light jacket over a loose t-shirt and leggings. She decides to head to the park while it's not raining; she has plenty of time to try to get know the locals.

She wonders if David thought that way, that he had plenty of time. She realises we haven't got all the time in the world like we tell ourselves sometimes and some of us will have a lot less than others.

It's just after nine am and the only people around seem to be people walking their dogs. The play area is almost empty apart from a couple of tired looking mothers with younger children who are not in school yet. She spots Jerry, the guy who lives across the road, sitting on a bench, watching his dog run around on the grass. She takes a seat next to him, seizing the opportunity to introduce herself.

'Hi,' she says, smiling in her usually friendly manner. 'I'm Lizzy, I just moved in across the street from you.'

'Oh, hello,' says Jerry, turning to take a look at her, but keeping a close eye on his beloved golden retriever. 'In David's old house you mean, is it?'

'Yes, that's right. I have heard all the stories about it being haunted,' she says with a small laugh, like she's expecting that to be the first thing he says. 'It doesn't scare me though.'

'Well, you're a brave girl then,' replies Jerry. 'I'm not sure I believe it anyway. He was a nice guy though, I think. Always had time to stop and say hello to Frank and me.'

'Frank is your dog?' asks Lizzy.

'Yes, the big, soft-looking one over there. He's only two years old, so still a puppy basically.'

'I think he's trying to impress the King Charles he's playing with,' says Lizzy.

'He'll wear himself out soon enough. That one looks more energetic than him.' He watches Frank, and his loud laugh is infectious.

'Do you know my neighbour, the lady with the red hair?' asks Lizzy. 'I'm not quite sure what to make of her yet. I've only seen her going in and out of the house.'

'That's the one with the facial expression that could curdle milk, is it?'

Lizzy can't help but let out a little snort of laughter, but Jerry continues.

'I'm not sure about her either,' he says. 'She's not very friendly with anyone from what I can tell.'

'Hmm, maybe I'll avoid making any effort with her at the minute then. What about the rest of the street? Anyone in particular I should avoid?'

Jerry watches Frank while thinking.

'Not really. Most are okay, I think. There's a few old nosy

ones, but they're harmless. If anything, they would probably tell you to avoid me,' he says, laughing that big laugh again. 'They'd say I'm grumpy and rude, no doubt.'

'I don't think that's true, Jerry. I wouldn't believe it.'

'It can be, but it depends on who I'm talking to. I never mean any harm, though. Life's too short. Oh, meet Frank,' he says as Frank runs over to them clumsily, his legs not quite cooperating with his brain.

'Hi, Frank,' says Lizzy, softly stroking his head, his tail wagging like it has its own energy source separate from the rest of his body.

Jerry takes a bottle of water and a dish out of a slightly worn-out backpack and puts some water down for Frank, which he shares with his little King Charles friend. They both lap it up like it's the last water they'll ever have, losing most of it out of the sides of their mouths. Lizzy loves dogs, but she thinks they need more attention than cats. At the moment, Frank is her new favourite dog, and his owner is her favourite neighbour. They walk back home together, and Lizzy feels like she's made her first friend on her street.

*

As Lizzy enters the living room and puts her keys down on the table, a movement in the corner of her eye catches her attention. David is here. She tries not to smile, even though she has no idea why she's so happy to see him. It's strange how she seems to feel more comfortable around this ghost than anyone else at the moment, even though she hasn't even spoken to him yet.

David is sitting on his chair, silently watching her, a curious expression on his face, like he's still unsure if she's aware of his presence or not. It's time to end the speculation.

'I know you're there,' says Lizzy, turning to meet his gaze.

'Yes, I can see you. I saw you when I was viewing the place, but I think you knew that.'

David doesn't look taken aback at all, maintaining his calm composure.

'I wasn't sure,' he replies. 'I didn't want to startle you. I never know who can see or hear me and who can't. You're the only one I've spoken to though since…' he trails off.

'Some of the kids around here say they've seen you looking out the window, but they could just be saying that to scare people.'

'Oh, they have seen me, or it seems that way. I do look out the window sometimes, but maybe they just see the curtains move or my breath on the window. I'm not actually sure.'

David pauses, taking in Lizzy. He stares a lot, which you would think would make Lizzy feel uncomfortable, but oddly enough, it doesn't.

'Aren't you afraid of me?' asks David.

'Not really,' says Lizzy a little too confidently. 'Should I be?'

'No, not at all,' he replies quickly. 'And I can go away if you want me to. I just…'

'You just what?' asks Lizzy.

'I heard you say that you're a writer. I'd love you to write my story about what happened to me.'

Lizzy has heard a little about what happened to David. When she was doing some research on the area, she stumbled upon a couple of news articles about it.

'Do you know what happened to you?' she asks. 'I read about it not long ago. It was a hit-and-run, wasn't it? But nobody was found, and it was assumed that it was an accident, that the driver panicked and drove off.'

'That's not what I believe happened,' says David calmly. 'That's where I was hoping you would come in, to hear my story and write about it. It might be a good idea for your first book? We would be the only ones who know it's based on a true story.'

Lizzy paces a little, arms folded, contemplating David's proposal.

'I have a lot of notes written down already,' he continues. 'There's some notebooks in that box in the bedroom, the one that has my name on it. Just be careful with the embossed one, please, the one with a phoenix on the cover. It was a gift from my grandmother; it's very old. I thought you could read through the notes and see what you think? I didn't want to forget any small details that might be worth mentioning.'

Lizzy stops pacing and faces David again, who eagerly waits for her reply.

'Okay, I'll take a look at the notebooks, but not right now.' She explains her parents will be there any minute with Tilly and that she needs him to disappear for a bit while they're there.

'Why?' he asks. 'They won't be able to see me anyway.'

'I know that, but I want some privacy while they're here. I don't want you listening in on conversations with my parents. Actually, I don't want you here when I have any company at all,' says Lizzy, gesturing to the living room door.

'You're right,' says David, rising from his chair. 'I'm sorry, I didn't think of it that way. I can go upstairs and put music on to block out the sound, if you'd like?' He smirks as Lizzy is about to react, then realises he's joking.

'Not funny, David. You can go upstairs if you want to, anywhere out of ear shot, but no music.' Lizzy feels a little less confident standing so close to him. He's always been sitting in his chair when she's seen him before, but now he towers over her.

'I had you pegged as a dog person, by the way,' he says.

'Dogs need more attention than cats. I work from home, so I need to focus and not be distracted every two minutes,' she says, before gesturing towards the door again, a little more impatiently this time.

'And cats don't cause distractions? I never had one, so I wouldn't know.'

'They can, but not as much. They say cats sense things; I wonder if she'll sense you here.'

'That could be fun,' he says with a questionable smile and raised eyebrow.

'Don't you dare try scaring her,' says Lizzy firmly, although her feeling of ease around David is starting to waiver now that she's spoken to him a little. 'She's from a shelter, and they don't know if she had a bad time before she went there. Am I clear?'

David nods.

'Good. Please can you leave now?' she says.

'Okay, okay, I'm going. I was only joking, by the way,' he says as he leaves the room. 'You can be quite scary when you want, can't you?'

Lizzy finds this all so surreal, the way they're chatting like they've known each other for years. She's not quite sure what to make of him after speaking to him. He has a friendly smile and kind eyes, but something about the way he stood towering over her, the little smirk when joking about the cat, makes her feel less comfortable around him than she did. She's interested to hear his story though and potentially get a plot for her first novel.

'Take a look at the notes whenever you're ready,' he says on his way up the stairs. 'It'll give you an idea of what you're getting into before you agree. And by the way, that painting on the wall doesn't look right there. I think you should get rid of it.'

Lizzy rolls her eyes and yells up the stairs after him.

'I will take a look at your notes, but the painting stays,' she says, looking at it fondly. 'It makes the room feel more homely.'

*

A knock at the door makes Lizzy jump out of her thoughts. She realises that it's probably her parents and rushes to the door in excitement to see Tilly.

'Hi,' squeals Lizzy, to her parents, but mostly to Tilly, who's timidly curled up in her carry crate. 'Thanks so much for picking her up.'

She stands back to let them in and hurries them into the living room, excited to let Tilly out to explore her new home. Tilly immediately walks over to Lizzy as she kneels on the floor to greet her properly. Lizzy picks her up for a cuddle before letting her down to check out all the furniture. She wanders around the sofa, the coffee table, and David's old armchair, before settling down on the TV unit.

That's a strange place for comfort Lizzy thinks, but Tilly seems happy so she leaves her to it.

'Are you going to be okay with her?' asks Lizzy's mother with a worried expression.

'Of course, Mam, why wouldn't I be?' replies Lizzy. 'She'll be good company for me. You worry too much, we'll be fine. She probably feels a bit overwhelmed with us all here.'

'And that's a hint for us to leave, Annie,' says Ron.

'You don't have to go, Dad. I didn't mean it like that,' says Lizzy unconvincingly.

'It's okay, love. We have to get back anyway, and the traffic was bad on the way here as usual.'

'It's always the same around here,' says Annie. 'I wish you'd moved somewhere less busy.'

'But then there's less people around,' replies Lizzy. 'You always said I'd be safer surrounded by people, not being too far out of the way.'

'I just meant a quiet neighbourhood, not on a farm somewhere alone.'

'Okay, well, I like it here,' says Lizzy defiantly.

'Okay, well, I guess maybe you'll be fine here,' says Annie hesitantly, gazing at Lizzy's new painting.

It's rare for Annie to let anything go when it comes to Lizzy and her safety, but Lizzy's not going to question her abrupt change of tune.

After what feels like an age, Annie and Ron leave Lizzy and Tilly alone. Lizzy curls up on the sofa with her for a while watching TV and Tilly nuzzles right in, purring like a motorbike.

Lizzy wakes up confused in the now darkening living room. She must have fallen asleep. There's very little light left coming through the window. She moves away from Tilly quietly and feels that chill you get after being still for so long then getting up. She turns on the light and closes the curtains, making sure to leave no gaps again. It's too early for dinner yet, so she tries to decide what to do for the next hour or so. She remembers David's notebooks in the box upstairs and decides to take a quick look at them now.

She looks around for him as she walks up the stairs and enters the bedroom, but he's nowhere to be seen. He told her where the notebooks are anyway and she thinks she remembers seeing them when she moved in. There was a box with his name on it and since he was still hanging around she thought she'd keep hold of it in case there was anything he wanted inside.

She opens the box and picks up the first notebook with a lovely, embellished cover and a picture of a phoenix.

When she opens it up, the pages are full of notes but they have been scribbled over with the words 'KILL HER' in large letters, repeated over and over on every page.

A feeling of panic settles in her stomach, her throat feels

constricted. Maybe she's got David wrong after all. This looks like it's been written by a psychopath.

For the first time, she feels afraid of David and the situation she's gotten herself in. She stands up quickly and moves under the light to take a better look at the notebooks but there's no doubting what it says. She realises there's so little she really knows about David, only what he's told her himself and what Jerry said, but Jerry didn't know him that well either.

Lizzy wonders about the lady next door, whether she knew him at all. She doesn't seem like the type to make friends with her neighbours but you never know; she seems like her only option right now. Lizzy just wants to get out of the house, but she can't tell her parents about this. Her instincts are telling her to get out of there right now.

She tries to go over everything quickly in her head. How could she have been so wrong? She replays the day she viewed the place in her head. Was he luring her in by staying silent, trying to make her feel sorry for him by appearing calm and pensive? The poor guy who got murdered so young. He was being so nice to her at first, making her feel comfortable around him. She's furious with herself for letting her guard down so easily. She wonders if this is what he was like before he died too. Feeling so disappointed in herself, she gets out of the room, runs down the stairs, and makes a quick exit straight out the front door, grabbing a jacket off the rack quickly as she passes.

She doesn't know if she's shivering with the cold or with fear as she knocks on her neighbour's door. She sees a blur of red hair making her way towards her through the frosted glass window. The lady pauses, as though hesitating, and then opens the door carefully, much to Lizzy's relief.

'Hi, I'm Lizzy from next door,' she says, trying to remain calm, flashing that winning friendly smile of hers.

'Hi,' replies the lady, looking around behind Lizzy as though checking if anyone else is there with her. 'I'm Chloe.'

'It's nice to meet you,' replies Lizzy. 'This may seem a bit odd, but I was wondering if you have a minute for me to ask you some questions about the guy who used to live in my house? His name was David?'

Lizzy thinks she sees Chloe's eyes widen with fear for the quickest second, before regaining her steady composure. She must know something.

Chloe looks around again, eyes darting up and down the street, then eyeing Lizzy up and down.

'Okay, come in,' she says finally, stepping back for Lizzy to enter her home. Lizzy breathes a sigh of relief and thanks her as she walks in. She stands at the end of the hallway and Chloe gestures for her to take a seat in the living room. The décor couldn't be more different to Lizzy's house. Bold colours, clashing patterns, nothing plain or simple about it. Lizzy takes a seat on the leather sofa, unsure how to hold her body or where to look. Chloe still stands in the doorway, making Lizzy feel even more uncomfortable.

'Do you want a cup of tea? Or a coffee?' she asks Lizzy.

'Oh, I'm okay, thank you,' says Lizzy, immediately regretting her answer. She could really do with a hot drink to warm the chill she got either from stepping outside or from what she saw in that notebook.

Chloe joins her on the sofa and there's an awkward pause where Lizzy doesn't quite know how to begin the conversation. Thankfully, Chloe breaks the silence for her.

'So, what did you want to know?' she asks. 'Do you know anything about him at all?'

'Not really,' replies Lizzy. 'I've heard about how he was killed in a hit and run accident, some of the neighbours have told me he was a nice guy and some of them say he haunts my house.'

Chloe laughs, but nervously. 'Does he?' she asks.

'Not yet,' Lizzy jokes back. She doesn't want Chloe to think she's completely crazy.

'I guess a lot of people thought he was a nice guy,' says Chloe, dragging her words out a little, like they're hard for her to stay.

'But you didn't?'

She looks at Lizzy like she's trying to suss out whether she can be trusted or not.

'We were friends for a while,' she says quickly and quietly, looking away from Lizzy. Lizzy's surprised by that. David didn't say he was friends with her.

'He was fine at first. Nicest guy you could ever meet, actually, but then...I don't know, he got a bit weird. He was pushy, coming around late, uninvited, usually drunk. Anyway, one night, as I was coming in from the kitchen, I saw him routing around my bookshelves. And not just looking at the books, like moving things around. He didn't hear me coming, so I backed up a little to try to see what he was doing. The way he was acting gave me a bad feeling, so I said I had a migraine coming on and I needed to go to bed, told him we'd do something another night instead. I just wanted him out of my house. He looked offended but he went. I checked the shelves as soon as he left, and I found a mini camera in between two books. It was so small, I don't think I would have noticed it if I hadn't been looking for it. I panicked, searched the rest of the house, and found another one in my bedroom. I couldn't find anymore, but I still felt like I was being watched all the time, and I couldn't shake it off. I still feel like that sometimes, and then I just have to remind myself that he's gone.'

The fear has truly set in now. Lizzy doesn't want to go home, but she can't tell Chloe why because Chloe will probably think she's insane. On the off chance Chloe does believe her, Lizzy doesn't want to put that fear back into her that David might show up at any second or still be watching her all the time.

'Rumour is that some girl he'd scared hit him with her car because she would rather he was dead than have to look over her shoulder forever. I can understand where she's coming from,' says Chloe, looking away. 'Look, if you ever get spooked in there, you're always welcome to stay here for the night. We women have to stick together, don't we?'

Chloe puts her hand on Lizzy's reassuringly, and Lizzy wants to tell her everything and stay here, but she knows she can't.

'Thanks, but I should be getting back,' she says reluctantly. 'I just found a few old things of David's that made me wonder, that's all.'

Chloe doesn't seem completely convinced that Lizzy is telling her everything.

'Well, I'm right here if you need anything,' she says.

Lizzy leaves, thanking Chloe for her time, and they both say goodnight.

*

While Lizzy is at Chloe's house, Clara waits for David to return. She knows what he's up to, what he's really like. She's been keeping a close eye, and she's not going to let him hurt Lizzy. She doesn't know what power he has over anyone as a ghost, but she has to get him out of here.

When David returns, he checks the downstairs rooms for Lizzy, wondering if she's been upstairs yet. When he enters the living room, a woman's voice screams 'GET OUT' so loud that he quickly covers his ears with his hands. For a predator, David looks awfully scared. He steps backwards, almost falling over the coffee table behind him. He looks around for the source of the voice, but there's no one here. His eyes fall on the painting, where the voice seemed to come from. He hears a giggle from the same direction and freezes.

'NOT SUCH THE TOUGH GUY NOW, ARE YOU? GET OUT OF HERE, WHILE YOU STILL CAN. IF YOU COME BACK, I WILL FIND AND KILL YOUR FAMILY.'

She expects him to run away in fear and shock, but he doesn't. Instead, he just simply disappears before her eyes. She waits, half-expecting him to pop up elsewhere, but the sense of his presence has gone. She thought he would have put up more of a fight, but when it comes down to it, he's just a coward. Clara feels confident David won't be back, not while she's around anyway.

*

Lizzy stands outside her front door for a while, trying to digest what Chloe told her. She doesn't know what to do. She wants to kick herself for being so stupid.

'It'll be fun moving into a haunted house,' she says under her breath, mocking herself. 'Stupid idiot.'

Anyway, Tilly is inside, and Lizzy doesn't want to leave her with David, so she has to suck it up and brave whatever is waiting for her inside.

She opens the door slowly, listening for signs of David. Everything seems quiet and still. She quietly and slowly walks up the stairs to find the box still on the floor where Lizzy left it, but now it's closed. She picks it up, her hands shaking slightly, and picks up the notebook she looked at earlier. Flicking through the pages, she realises it's all different. She flips back to the cover, checking it's the right one. She glances back at the box to check it's the only one with the phoenix on the cover. Where 'KILL HER' was written over and over on the pages, it now says 'HE'S

GONE'. She pauses, listening and looking around the house. For a reason she can't quite understand, she believes that David is gone. The atmosphere in the house has changed; everything feels oddly calm.

*

Everything that's happened in the last twenty-four hours hits Lizzy at once, and she has to step back to take a seat on the bed. She's gone from finding what she believed to be a friend in David, wanting to hear his story and help him, to finding out that he was actually a dangerous person to be around. Yet, for some reason, she feels alone again. She tries to look for the silver lining in all of this. It'll be easier to write her book now without the distraction of a ghost popping up every now and then, and she definitely has some good material to work into her story now.

She walks back downstairs, makes herself a cup of tea, and joins Tilly on the sofa. Tilly seems so unbothered by anything that's gone on, like she hasn't even noticed. Tilly is all the company Lizzy needs for now. She still feels a little uneasy, her hands still trembling slightly at the thought of David popping up out of nowhere all of a sudden, and she's puzzled by what she found in the notebook. Who would have written 'he's gone'? Maybe it was David, and he had a good side and bad side that he was battling with. She can't think of any other explanation. Tilly stares at the painting hanging on the wall, drawing Lizzy's eyes to it. A sense of calm washes over her like someone is trying to tell her she's safe now.

*

Chloe knocks on Lizzy's door the next morning to check that Lizzy's okay. She couldn't get their conversation out of her head all night.

'I was just wondering if you'd like to maybe get some breakfast? There's a nice café just around the corner?'

Lizzy gets the feeling Chloe doesn't invite people to do anything with her often. She avoids eye contact and shuffles her feet, her usually confident demeanour falling away. Lizzy can't help but smile.

'I'd love to. Let me just grab a jacket.'

The walk there is slightly awkward, but Lizzy is good at making small talk and making people feel comfortable in her presence.

As they eat, Lizzy decides Chloe is safe to open up to and reveals the truth about what really happened with David—about his ghost hanging around and him wanting her to write his story.

Chloe is dismissive at first, as though she thinks Lizzy is playing some kind of joke on her, but then she can see a hint of fear still lingering in Lizzy's eyes, the trauma of it all still on her face. Chloe looks terrified when she first starts to believe what Lizzy's saying, and Lizzy has to reassure her over and over that he really is gone.

They go back to Lizzy's after breakfast, where she shows Chloe the notebooks. They burn them in Lizzy's backyard, removing every trace of David's life and death that remained in the house.

Later that night, Lizzy finds a new notebook she hasn't seen before. The handwriting isn't David's though, and it's nothing to do with his story; it has a different story in it, one she hasn't read before. It's the story of a young woman who was betrayed by her husband. The woman left him and lived alone with her despair and her rage for the rest of her life. Lizzy reads it all in one go, unable to put it down. This is the story she'll write, but maybe in Lizzy's version, the young woman will get her happy ending. David doesn't deserve to have anything written about him.

It takes a while before Lizzy can sleep again without leaving a lamp on or having bad dreams, seeing David's body hovering over her while she sleeps or lurking behind a door when she enters a room. She stays at Chloe's some nights, when it gets too much and she needs some company. Chloe even stays at Lizzy's sometimes, and Lizzy loves that she feels safe to do that after everything. They're like therapy for each other, helping each other get over all the bad memories of David and what he could have done to them. Chloe may even tell Lizzy one day that she was the one who took matters into her own hands.

Clara

Clara had never considered that she might be able to scare a ghost until David came along. She scared herself a little, letting that old part of her out again. She knew she had to act quickly to save Lizzy. She had to keep a close eye and find out David's weakness, which turned out to be his family. He was so clever and convincing at playing the nice guy, he even had Clara fooled at the beginning.

Lizzy went on to marry Chloe's brother, so now they are family for real. When Jerry sadly passed not too long later, Lizzy took Frank in as per Jerry's wish, and her once quiet home became full of love and laughter with her two daughters, Frank, and, of course, Tilly. It was quite a houseful, never a quiet moment, and Lizzy couldn't have been happier.

By that point, Clara had been confined to her painting for so long that she had seen so many things happen and watched as the world continued to change. She started to feel like she was the cursed one. She used to look at new things in the world and think how wonderful it would have been to have them in her time, but things seemed to take a turn in the wrong direction. New technology had started creeping in—things that she saw as potential dangers for the future.

As soon as the new technology started, it seemed to snowball so quickly. Clara struggled to keep up with all the changes and it made her feel old and tired.

After Lizzy, Clara found a new home in a garden shed belonging to a little girl named Mia. Mia hadn't had a normal childhood so far, not like anything Clara had seen before.

It made Clara think of her own daughter and how glad she was that she had gotten to grow up when she did, when children could play freely in the streets and explore the world and be mischievous. She hoped that Eliza had gotten to experience that kind of childhood.

Though Clara never talked to her parents about Eliza, she found a photograph of her one day in her mother's bag and took it. She kept it in a drawer in her bedroom. She rarely looked at it, but she felt better knowing it was there. Eliza didn't resemble Jack much at all; she was all Clara.

Clara left a note for Eliza before she died.

'My darling Eliza, I can never apologise enough for abandoning you the way I did. I hope you know that I did it with the very best intentions for you. I hope you had a good life. I'm sure it was better than any life I could have given you. I understand if you can never forgive me, but my house and money are yours if you would like them. You can take anything you want, except the painting. Take the painting to an auction or market immediately. It will bring you bad luck if you keep it.'

Eliza did as her mother had instructed and took it to a shop, where it was bought by Charles.

Monica & Erik

Monica renovated the shed for her daughter, Mia, a few years back, transforming it into a real-life fairytale room. Flowerpots with different coloured roses decorate the windowsills and the bookshelves that line the walls, along with old ornaments passed down through generations and a collection of family photos. Two child-sized armchairs sit in the corner, almost facing each other, reupholstered by Monica with a multi-coloured floral material. The pastel green curtains match the colour of the walls outside. A painting hangs on the wall that Monica tried to talk Mia out of, insisting that it didn't really go with the rest of the room, but Mia was adamant that the painting belonged in the shed. The painting, though incredibly detailed and mesmerising in a way Monica can't quite put her finger on, shows a family playing together on the beach. It's a nice painting, but it looks out of place amongst the florals and pastels, and Monica can't help thinking it's a strange choice for a child of nine years old.

Last year, they had to remove the books from the shelves and hide them under the bench seats that Monica installed in the shed. A new law had been passed stating that any books that were not AI-generated were banned, meaning every book written by a human was to be confiscated and destroyed. Everything was being taken away from them slowly. Monica kept most of the children's classics, trying to accumulate a decent collection for Mia before they were all destroyed. She also wrote her own summarised versions in notebooks for Mia before they were forgotten forever. She kept some for herself too, with the intention of passing them down to Mia when she's old enough to read them—some of Monica's favourites that she couldn't bear to part with, books that didn't deserve to never be read again, like Cleopatra and

Frankenstein, The One, and Normal People. Monica didn't want Mia to never get to experience the wonderful, magical wording of Coco Mellors or experience the cleverness of a John Marrs book. As for Normal People, Monica isn't sure whether anyone will ever have that kind of normal again. She wants people to remember how things used to be; maybe it will make people want to fight for everything that's being taken away.

The books have all been moved to the attic now, stored under a couple of loose floorboards hidden beneath an old dusty rug, mostly in an attempt to avoid them being found and confiscated during one of the routine house searches, but also to keep them out of the hands of Mia and her curious mind. Monica found her one day sitting on her bedroom floor with a thriller open in her lap. Luckily, she was only a couple of pages in. Mia knew she was in trouble; she knew she was too young to read her mother's books.

Monica tries hard to nurture Mia's curious and inquisitive mind, but it doesn't come easy with so much being taken away from them. Mia gets bored of the bland AI books; reading one of those is like eating a cake without sugar or trying to smell flowers with no scent.

At school, children sit at computers all day, learning only how to be a part of this new world. They rarely go outside, and communication with other children is limited. Monica tries to teach Mia the important stuff at home—about science, nature, and humanity. Erik, Monica's husband, tries to help when he can, but he works a lot providing admin services for a security company. He doesn't enjoy it as much as his old job, but it pays the bills, and choices are limited now. He used to design new homes, but that's all done by AI now too. The hours are long and he only gets Sundays off, so Mia likes to spend as much time as she can with him in the evenings, and Monica works hard to make sure they make the most of the time they do spend together as a family. Monica doesn't work anymore; there aren't many jobs to go around these days, but the ones that are available pay better at least, so that households can manage on one income. Mia never wants for anything, but what she needs is no longer allowed. Things like human connection and real books and movies. Most of the classic children's movies were deemed no longer suitable; anything with a 15-year-old rating was banned, and some with a 12-year-old rating were too. Comedies are no longer funny, and action films are non-stop over-the-top stunts created with a computer instead of stuntmen and film crews. Even sports are not the same, and Erik deeply misses the old versions that he used to watch with his dad when he was young. Anyone watching motor sports in the past would probably never imagine watching a car race with a speed limit, but that's how it is now.

Monica and Erik tried to hang onto some of their old DVD's, but they were found during a random search one day and taken away to be destroyed. The searches are less frequent now that so much has been confiscated, but you never know when they'll turn up at the front door. The books in the shed always go under the seats in concealed cupboards, but they'll probably find those one day, along with the books in the attic.

Decorating the shed also helped take Monica's mind off her sister, Melissa, a little bit. Melissa went missing a couple of months ago along with a few others; she told Monica that there was a group of people getting together to try to fight against the changes, but that it would take a long time to plan everything properly. Monica wishes Melissa had stayed out of it all; she worries about her all the time. Melissa, strong-willed and determined as always, insisted that she would be fine and that Monica would thank her for it one day, but Monica knows how easily led her younger sister can be sometimes and can't help but have a bad feeling about all of it.

*

Monica makes her way down to the kitchen for her morning coffee in her fluffy slippers and cosy dressing gown. The mornings are getting colder now as they head towards winter. The tree in the back garden has lost most of its leaves already, a carpet of brown and orange on the ground around the base of the trunk.

Erik is already busy working in his office upstairs, and Mia is out in the shed. They're always up before Monica; she finds it harder to get out of bed now that she has no job to go to, and every day is much the same as the one before. Mia's off school for half term, so Monica lets her do as she pleases for the mornings, which usually involves reading or playing in her shed. They used to watch TV together every morning during the school holidays, but now they can never find anything remotely interesting to watch. Monica's been giving Mia extra lessons while they have the time, which Mia actually seems to enjoy.

Monica wraps her dressing gown a little tighter around herself and heads down the path to the shed to call Mia in for breakfast. The wind is relentless, and she holds the collar of her dressing gown up around her ears until she reaches the door. She reaches for the door handle but then stops when she hears Mia laughing from inside.

'That's quite funny,' says Mia. 'What happened next?'

Monica's first thought is that Erik must be in there with her, but she swears she heard him talking on the phone as she walked by his office five minutes ago. She pulls the handle down and enters the shed. Mia looks startled, and her cheeks turn slightly pink.

'Mum, you scared me,' she says quietly.

Monica looks around the shed to find that Mia is in there alone.

'Sorry, love, I didn't mean to scare you. Who were you talking to?' she asks, still looking around even though it's an open-plan room, and if there was someone else in here, she would be able to see them immediately.

'Nobody, I was reading,' says Mia, holding up a worn and faded copy of Charlotte's Web.

'Oh right, sorry. I thought maybe Dad was in here with you.'

Monica knows some parts of Charlotte's Web can be funny, but Mia's read it so many times now, she's not convinced that's what she was laughing at. Maybe she was talking to herself and got embarrassed. Monica tries to move past it.

'Are you coming in for some cereal?' she asks Mia.

'Can I finish this chapter first?' says Mia, still looking a little embarrassed.

'Okay,' says Monica, nodding. She leaves but hovers by the door slightly after closing it before continuing back up the path.

'That was close,' says Mia quietly.

Monica gets an uneasy feeling in her stomach, but she tries to brush past it as she gets to the kitchen and starts preparing breakfast. Maybe Mia has invented an imaginary friend, or she could just be role playing, acting as a teacher, or something.

Monica gets a dish of Weetabix ready on the table for Mia. She likes the milk to soak into them until they're soggy. Monica pours her coffee and butters her toast, then sits at the table as Mia comes in to join her.

She doesn't question Mia about what happened in the shed and puts it down to Mia just playing.

Monica turns on the radio so she can listen to the news

while they eat. They're discussing art again, specifically what the rules should be for what is allowed and what should be destroyed. She can't wrap her head around how many people side with the government on these things. Mia frowns and looks up at Monica.

'Will we have to get rid of our painting in the shed?' she asks.

'I don't know,' says Monica, unable to hide the disappointment in her voice at what the world has come to me. 'Maybe.'

'But we keep our books. Can't we keep the painting?'

'Well, we'll try to hang on to it as long as we can, just like the books. It's harder to hide a painting than a book, though.'

Mia looks concerned. Monica hates having to take these things away from her.

'Clara says she doesn't want to leave,' says Mia suddenly and defiantly. 'She's my friend.'

Monica pauses with her slice of toast almost to her mouth, then puts it back on the plate and tries to keep her voice steady.

'Who's Clara, honey?'

'The lady who lives in my painting. She talks to me about old books and old places she lived in,' says Mia, her voice getting higher and tears building up in her eyes.

'Mia, people don't live in paintings,' says Monica softly, reaching her hand over and placing it on top of Mia's. 'Do you imagine her?'

Mia pulls her hand away, but then her face softens, and her voice returns to its normal tone.

'No, I see her. She's pretty; she's got long black hair and a nice smile. She's kind and says she lived in some really good times, better than now. She used to have a farm where she kept chickens and pigs, like Wilbur.'

'Okay, well, do you think she would let me see her too?'

asks Monica.

'Not yet,' says Mia, shaking her head. 'I already asked her, and she said maybe one day. She said I can see her because I'm clever.'

Monica's not really sure how to deal with this. She'll have to talk to Erik about it later, when he finishes work. She can understand why anyone would want to make up a friend in these times, especially a kid. They don't get to socialise as much as they used to without break times to play in the yard and with computer screens in their faces all day.

'Are you going back to the shed after breakfast or coming to watch a movie with me?' asks Monica, softly brushing Mia's hair behind her ears.

'Back to the shed,' says Mia with a mouthful of Weetabix. 'Clara can finish her story about her chickens.'

Monica smiles a tight-lipped smile, trying to hold it all in for now.

'Okay,' she says. 'Well, you and Clara have fun.'

*

After breakfast, Monica goes upstairs to get dressed and then knocks on Erik's office door.

'Come in,' he says in a formal tone, even though he knows it's probably Monica or Mia.

'What's up?' he asks as Monica enters, not taking his eyes off his computer screen.

Monica perches herself on the edge of his desk.

'Mia has an imaginary friend. Apparently her name is Clara. Should we be worried?' she asks, looking over the papers in the open file next to her on the desk.

'I'm not sure, what did she say exactly?' asks Erik, closing the file and moving it to the other side of his desk. 'You know all this stuff is confidential, babe,' he says apologetically.

Monica stands back up, a little embarrassed about always having to be reminded that he can't share any details of his work with anyone, not even his family.

'She said that Clara lives in the painting in the shed and talks to her about the past.'

Erik sits back in his leather desk chair, clasping his hands together in his lap.

'Well, at least she told you about it, so she's not uncomfortable talking about her. Maybe we should just let it run its course? Lots of kids have imaginary friends, don't they? Or I could talk to her about it later if you want, see if she says anything else.'

'No,' says Monica quickly. 'She might not trust me enough to tell me anything else if she knows I've spoken to you about it.' She walks over to the door and peers down the hallway, checking that Mia hasn't come back into the house and isn't listening.

'Okay, well, if you change your mind,' says Erik, leaning forward and turning his focus back to his computer screen.

'I'll let you get on,' says Monica. 'I need to do some washing anyway.'

She finds herself looking out the window down towards the shed more than she normally would this morning, expecting to see something, but she has no idea what. She's relieved when it's lunchtime and Mia comes back into the house.

Erik joins them briefly for lunch before heading down to the shed to make a phone call while Monica and Mia are still eating. Sometimes there are calls he can't make from the house due to the nature of his job. There are rules in place that state some phone calls need extra caution to avoid any risk of family members overhearing. Monica used to hate it, knowing that Erik could trust her with anything, but it's just something that she's gotten used to now. He reassures her constantly that he just wants to stick to the rules so he can keep his job; they're so hard to get these days, and Monica knows he's right.

Mia seems in better spirits than this morning and hasn't mentioned Clara at all while they eat.

'Will you be giving me lessons today?' she asks Monica eagerly. 'Can we read? I want to finish Charlotte's Web'. There's always a barrage of questions strung together so that Monica doesn't have a chance to answer one before the next one comes out.

'Yes, if you want to. Just give me half an hour to tidy up and do some chores quickly,' says Monica.

'Okay. Can I take my crisps down to the shed to eat?' asks Mia.

'You can, but you'll have to wait until Dad's finished on his phone call first.'

'I know,' she says, rolling her eyes. 'I'm not stupid, Mum.'

Monica rests her hand on her hip and rolls her eyes back but smiles.

'You are cheeky though,' she says, and they both laugh. Monica feels sad sometimes thinking about how much Mia is missing out on. She should be out playing with friends today, but there aren't many places for kids to play anymore and not much left for them to play with.

Erik returns from the shed, shivering as he comes through the door. His dark, usually neatly combed hair is all in disarray from the wind. One brush through with his hand, and it's almost all back in place.

'It's biting out there today. You should put a jacket or coat on to go down there this afternoon, Mia,' he says.

'I know, Dad. I always do when it's cold, and I have the big blanket down there to put over me.'

Monica notices that Mia gets a little annoyed sometimes that Erik doesn't take much notice of what she does. He often tells her to do things that she already does; he's just too busy to notice.

'Okay, well, make sure you wrap up. I'll see you later.'

He leans over and kisses her on her forehead before heading back to his office. Mia quickly runs to get her coat.

'I'll be out soon, Mia,' Monica calls after her as she heads back down to the shed.

Monica turns towards the laundry basket and the pile of clothes within it and wonders, as she does every time, how they go through so many clothes in just a couple of days when there are only three of them and they hardly leave the house.

She organises them all into piles and puts them away, trying to be as quick as possible so she can go and read Charlotte's Web with Mia. It was one of her favourite books growing up; she's glad Mia seems to like it so much. She grabs two bars of chocolate from the cupboard, one for herself and one for Mia. She knows she shouldn't eat so many of them now that they're only allowed to buy so many a week, but she convinced Erik to let her buy his allowed amount too because he never eats them.

Her eyes move over to an old photo of the three of them together from last year. She always tries to figure out who Mia looks more like—her or Erik. They all have dark hair; Erik's is a little darker than Mia's and Monica's. Mia always likes to leave her long hair down, flowing freely, always refusing to let Monica tie it up or try out new hairstyles. Mia has Erik's hazelnut eyes and is tall like him too.

Erik used to shower Monica with attention until he took this job. Now they have very little time to themselves, and he seems to focus all his spare time on Mia, which still isn't enough. He still misses so much of her growing up, despite living in the same house. Monica shakes her head and puffs out a long breath, trying to rid herself of the longing for what used to be, then makes her way to shed.

*

Monica is greeted with a big, adoring smile from Mia when she joins her in the shed.

'It's so cold in here, Mia,' says Monica, wrapping her coat tighter around herself. 'Maybe we should go up to the house today.'

Mia stands up and gently takes Monica's hand, a serious look on her face all of a sudden.

'No, I'm okay,' she says, glancing to the painting on the wall and back at Monica. 'I know you don't believe me about Clara, but she said I have to go up to the house for ten minutes and give you this camera. She said you need to watch what's on it.'

She hands Monica the small device and lets go of her hand, ready to leave.

'What is it?' asks Monica.

Mia avoids Monica's eyes now, like she knows she's in trouble for something.

'Please don't be angry,' she says quickly. 'I only borrowed the camera out of Dad's office because I wanted to record myself reading. He showed me how to use it once, and I told Clara about it. She asked me to switch it on this morning, and she said you're the only one I can show it to. You plug it into your phone and press play.'

Mia quickly runs off up to the house, eager to avoid a telling-off for taking her dad's camera and any questions Monica might have about Clara.

Monica looks at the painting and then back to the camera. She does as Mia said and plugs it into her phone. Her eyebrows furrow as she tries to make sense of what she's watching.

The video shows Erik in the shed on the work call he made earlier today. He's wearing the same light blue shirt, and his hair is tousled from the wind. Monica turns up the volume and takes a seat on one of the benches. As she starts to make out what he's saying, her heart begins to race as she realises this isn't a work call.

'I'll leave a key under the plant pot outside the front door,' says Erik, talking quickly. 'I'll take Mia over to my parents' house. Monica always tries to get out of it so she'll be here alone. Yes, definitely. She never wants to come with us. She should be out cold by the time you get here. I'll put the stuff in her coffee and try to make sure I'm leaving not long after she drinks it. Don't forget to torch the shed as well as the house.' Erik stares at the painting. Monica can't see his face as the camera shows the back of his head, but she notices a shiver run through him. 'Make sure you burn that painting in the shed too. It gives me the creeps.'

Monica feels as though the ground is spinning beneath her, and she struggles to focus on the rest of the video.

'I'm not getting caught with all this illegal crap,' says Erik in a voice that sounds like someone else's. His tone softens. 'When things settle, we can finally be together properly. It feels like forever since I've seen you.'

Monica's hands start to shake, so she places the phone next to her and focusses on calming her now rapid heart rate. She takes a long, shaky breath in and out, knowing that Mia could come in at any minute, so she has to pull herself together. She tries to make sense of what she's just watched but she can't. She looks up at the painting and peers out the window to see if there's any sign of Mia, but she must still be in the house.

'Clara?' says Monica, her voice shaking, but there's no reply. She can't hold it in any longer. She feels like she's been punched in the chest, and she can't stop the tears coming. She sits on the bench and sobs into her hands.

'What's wrong, Mum?' comes Mia's soft voice from the doorway. 'Did Clara upset you? Did she do something bad?' She quickly walks over to Monica and perches herself on her lap, wrapping her arms behind her neck. 'I didn't mean to make you cry,' she says into Monica's hair.

Monica quickly tries to collect herself, wiping away her tears.

'No, Mia, you didn't make me cry. Clara didn't do anything. She just... she wanted to show me how good you are at reading while I'm not here, that's all.'

Monica tries to smile as Mia studies her face, confusion all over her own.

'Really? And that made you sad?'

'No, it made me so happy and proud that I started crying happy tears. I know, I'm so silly sometimes, aren't I?' She tries her best to smile and reassure Mia that everything is okay.

'Very silly, Mum,' says Mia, laughing as relief fills her face.

'Don't tell your dad though, okay? He really will think I've been silly, so it's just between me and you. And he wouldn't understand about Clara,' says Monica.

'Okay,' says Mia. 'I know he wouldn't anyway. He's taking me to Granny and Grampa's house tomorrow. Are you coming? Dad said you're not.'

'No, I've got so much cleaning to do, but I can make you a nice dinner ready for when you get back,' says Monica, her voice still trembling slightly.

'Okay,' says Mia, sliding off Monica's lap and picking up her copy of Charlotte's Web. 'Are we going to read now?'

'I tell you what, why don't you read to me for a while? Like you did when I wasn't here, and I can listen to how good you are for real. How's that sound?'

Monica needs time to think and go over what she's just heard on the video. Who could he be talking to? He hardly goes anywhere; how could he have met someone? She has so many questions that she doesn't know how to get the answers to.

Later in the evening, Erik asks Monica if she wants to go with him to visit his parents tomorrow, hoping she'll say no, as expected. She's tempted to say yes, just to see the look on his face and watch him try to talk her out of it, but she doesn't want to play games. She doesn't want to be near him at all right now.

*

Monica spent most of the night restless and dreading the morning. She's worried about Mia being with Erik today, but there's nothing she can do about that without him getting suspicious that she knows something. She thought about trying to run off with her, but where would they go? It would have to be somewhere Erik wouldn't find them, and she couldn't think of anywhere. She gets up and tries to act as normal as she possibly can.

Mia and Erik are already at the breakfast table, Mia's legs swinging happily, just too short to reach the floor, as she eats her cereal.

'Good morning,' says Erik, looking up from his phone and flashing a wide smile. Monica smiles back, but she struggles to speak. 'Sit down, I'll get you some coffee.'

She sits at the table, and Mia immediately starts talking to her, but Monica finds it hard to focus, keeping one eye on Erik. When her coffee is ready, Monica interrupts Mia mid-sentence.

'Why don't you go upstairs with Daddy and he can pick out something nice for you to wear to Gran's and Grampa's?' she says.

Erik places the coffee in front of Monica, smiling in a way

that makes her blood run cold.

'Thank you,' she says quietly, turning away from him.

'Come on then, Mia,' he says, watching Monica cautiously as they leave the room. She lifts the coffee mug to her lips as he's walking out of the door, knowing that he's watching to make sure she drinks it. When she hears him on the stairs, she quickly runs over to the sink and washes her mouth out. She doesn't know what he's put in the drink, and she doesn't want to risk it. She pours the rest down the sink, leaving just a small amount at the bottom of the cup as she always does, and sits back at the table, trying to stop herself fidgeting when they re-enter, all dressed and ready to go.

'Mum, do you like my dress?' asks Mia, doing a little twirl for her.

'You look so beautiful,' says Monica, and she feels tears rising in her eyes that she quickly tries to force away. Erik is watching her closely, looking for any signs of whatever he's giving her to take effect. He peers over at the mug on the kitchen counter, and she swears she sees him smile when he sees that the cup is almost empty.

'Well, we'll be back in a few hours,' he says, leaning over and kissing Monica on the forehead. It takes all of her energy not to push him away. She hugs Mia tighter than she normally would and walks to the front door to wave them off. Her stomach is a bunch of twisted knots seeing how happy Erik is this morning, knowing what he's doing, or what he thinks he's doing.

As soon as the door is closed, Monica runs to the cupboard under the stairs to grab a couple of boxes she's put ready. She takes them down to the shed and quickly starts throwing the books in, before taking them up to the attic. She takes the painting off the wall and takes that up too. As she places it in the corner of the attic, she takes a blanket to put over it and quietly whispers a thank you to Clara before covering it up.

She heads back downstairs and tries to steady her breathing after all the running around. Then she picks up her phone and calls the police, checking that everything is okay and the plan is still the same. She called them last night when Mia was asleep and Erik was still in his office. She told them all about the recording, and they quickly came up with a plan to stop Erik and stop any harm coming to Monica. They assure her that there are undercover officers outside keeping an eye on the house. They want whoever is going to turn up to come into the house so that they get caught in the act. Monica can't even take a guess at who it might be, but surely it has to be someone Erik works with. He doesn't talk to anyone else that she knows of, but then she doesn't know as much as she thought she did. She lays on the sofa and pretends to be unconscious, as instructed by the police officers. The culprit needs to think the plan is still going ahead and that Monica has been drugged. She focusses on steadying her breathing to a slower, deeper pace.

  As she hears the clicking of the front door opening, she feels her heart beating out of her chest. She keeps reassuring herself that everything will be fine; the police are watching. She just needs to keep as calm and still as possible. She hears footsteps approaching, slowly and carefully, getting closer and closer, until she can feel someone's breath on her face. They hover over her for a moment before walking away and making their way towards the back door. As the footsteps fade away into the garden, Monica slowly opens her eyes, trying to look around before moving, just in case. The back door has been left open, so Monica slowly gets off the sofa and moves to the edge of the patio doors, carefully peering out. She's disappointed to see that the person is wearing a hoodie with the hood up, and they have their back to her so she can't see their face. They have a small figure, which is a little less daunting. She quickly presses send on the message she had typed out earlier for the police officer, sending a signal for them to enter. Now that she knows help is coming quickly, she can't help herself. The hooded figure has entered the shed, and Monica follows them, picking up her pace as she gets closer, letting all the anger wash over her and move her forward. She pulls the door open hard, and they turn around and look straight at her.

Both of them freeze, and Monica can't believe what she's seeing, her brain unable to make the connections.

'Melissa?' she says. Monica's little sister stares at her, her eyes wide and startled. Monica's fear drains out of her, and she can't help but revert to her big sister tone. 'What are you doing?'

The little sister that she's been worried about for months, the one who was supposedly off plotting against the government, was apparently off plotting against Monica this whole time, with the help of Monica's husband. Her hands start to shake with rage as she realises what's happening, but there are footsteps in the garden, and a loud, stern voice shouts that Melissa should put her hands in the air. Monica watches, speechless, as Melissa's hands are placed behind her back and into cuffs as her rights are read to her. One of the officers asks Monica if she's hurt, but she can't take her eyes off her little sister, the one that used to sneak into her bed at night after a nightmare or ask her to braid her hair for school. The police walk Melissa past Monica, and she hears her own voice tremble as she asks, 'Why would you do this?'

Melissa doesn't respond, she just stares right into her eyes, her face completely emotionless, and then she's walked away by the officers and doesn't look back.

The officer who asked if Monica was hurt ushers her back towards the house where Monica takes a seat on the sofa, still trying to process what's happened.

'We'll pick your husband up from his parent's house, so

you might want to follow on and get your daughter. We've taken the mug you left in the kitchen for forensics, and we've got a copy of the video you sent us. They'll both be going away for a long time for attempted murder,' says the officer confidently.

'Thank you,' says Monica quietly, 'for everything.' Thank you doesn't seem enough for all they've done, but she doesn't know what else to stay. She gets her keys and follows the officers out of the house. She watches as they put Melissa in the back of their car, too many mixed thoughts and emotions flowing through her. She tries to ignore the neighbours peeking from behind their curtains or blatantly standing out on the doorstep trying to figure out what's happened. She dreads to think of the stories they'll come up with, but wonders how those stories could possibly be worse than the truth. She thinks of Mia and how she could possibly explain any of this to her. The weight of telling her that her dad will no longer be around and building a new life for the two of them makes her body feel heavy. How do you come back from having your life shattered by two of the people you loved the most?

*

It's been two weeks since Erik and Melissa were arrested. Neither of them got bail. Monica tried to explain to Mia what happened in a way that wasn't too much for her, but it wasn't easy. She's finding it hard and missing her dad, but Monica keeps a close eye on her, and she knows that Mia talks to Clara often. Monica is so grateful to Clara, whoever and whatever she is, and she lets Mia have the time to talk to her, knowing that it's probably easier for her to talk to Clara.

Monica was lucky enough to find a job that she can do from home and pays enough to keep them in their house. She still worries about the painting and everything else getting discovered and taken away. She set up a small reading nook in the attic instead, where Clara hangs low on the wall. Hopefully, she's safer there.

Monica doesn't know if she'll ever be able to move on from the betrayal of her own sister and husband. She visited Melissa once to try to make sense of it all, but it did no good. Monica didn't recognise the person sitting behind the glass; it was like she was talking to a stranger. Mia tells Monica that Clara says she'll move on in time and meet someone else, someone kind. That's easy for Clara to say, Monica thinks. She's not just been cheated on by her husband, who then planned to have her killed by her own sister. If she had, then maybe she would understand a little better.

Clara

Clara spent many years in that home, hidden away in the attic. Mia continued to sit with Clara and speak to her, even when she had moved out and had a family of her own. Any time she visited Monica, she visited Clara too.

Monica was reluctant to let anyone else in their lives after what Erik did, but eventually she met a man who made her feel so safe and loved that she couldn't ignore it. She lived a long life and died peacefully in her sleep, after spending decades participating in the fight against the new laws. She fought with many others for their freedom.

After Monica passed, Mia sold the house to a couple named Alfie and Freya. Their teenage son, Liam, lived with them also, and their daughter, Lori, lived with her husband closer to the city. Lori had been struggling deeply with the restrictions that had been placed on their lives. Despite the fight people had been putting up, the laws had continued to spiral out of control. Alfie and Freya had tried to bring their children up in a world that was as normal as they could make it, instilling old values and teaching them how things used to be. Lori desperately longed for that kind of life. She was one of the saddest people Clara had come across but also one of the most hopeful and determined for change.

Clara compared her old life to Lori's, and the difference was immense. It was as though they had lived on different planets. Clara reminisced about the simple things like going for walks around her farm and the fields, the smell of nature all around her, picking flowers, the damp smell that followed a rain shower after a long spell of dry weather and the sound of dogs barking and children laughing as they ran and played outside. It was a much simpler and much more beautiful time. Clara couldn't help but feel she had taken her life and what she had for granted as she watched Lori and Elliot live like prisoners in their own home.

Clara was discovered in the attic one day by Alfie and Freya. She thought she would be demolished, that the laws were getting too strict to be ignored, and people wouldn't want to risk keeping her painting, but she wasn't. She was gifted to Lori and hidden away again. Clara wondered if she would be confined to attics for the rest of her days. When Freya tried to trace where the painting had come from, she discovered that it had once belonged to a distant grandparent of hers, a woman named Eliza. Clara had returned home.

Lori & Elliot

Lori pins the brooch her father gave her onto her t-shirt, smiling fondly at the reflection of it in the mirror as she does so. He found it in the attic of their new home a couple of years ago. It's simple and delicate, nothing extravagant or fancy about it, but Lori loves the way the multi-coloured stones sparkle, especially the ruby one in the middle. The surrounding colours complement it like twinkling stars around a dark red moon.

Her parents found a secret stash of now illegal items hidden away in the corner of their attic. Her father was eager to get rid of all of it, wanting to avoid any trouble, but her mother was keen to keep it all, pointing out that it all looked like it had been there for years anyway and hadn't been discovered yet. Lori's mother spent many evenings in the attic reading through an old book collection she found, getting lost in the kind of stories she remembered being fond of as a child. When she was moving things around one evening to make it a little more comfortable, she found a slightly faded but captivating painting hidden beneath a large blanket. She studied it for a while, taking in all the colours and details; it looked like it had faded over time, but there was still something quite mesmerising about it. After doing some research, she discovered that the painting had once belonged to a very distant relative of theirs and decided to pass it on to Lori. She knew it was something Lori would love.

She can't hang it on the wall, of course, so it's hidden away in her attic also, but she likes to look at it every now and then. She feels like she notices new details each time, something she hadn't noticed before. She feels like the painting knows somehow that she's breaking the law to keep it safe, a feeling she can't explain.

As she brushes her hair and gets ready to go downstairs for breakfast, she thinks about how much the world has changed in the last decade or so. Technology has a lot to answer for, or rather, the humans who are in charge and put too much faith in technology have a lot to answer for. Everyone saw the changes happening and just went along with it. Now here they are, in a mostly unrecognisable new world where they've been robbed of almost everything that made life good.

Lori's husband, Elliot, is making breakfast when she enters the kitchen. She sits on a stool by the kitchen island and watches him, a tea towel slung over his shoulder, whistling away like a perfect husband character from an old sitcom that would be banned now. His dark brown hair sits perfectly in place, the complete opposite of the longer, out-of-control wavy hair he had when they first met. Lori thinks it made him look younger like that, more relaxed and carefree. She used to look at him and see her soul mate, the fun guy who was always making her laugh. Now when she looks at him, she has a very clear image in her mind of an android from an old movie, saying what he thinks he should be saying, never questioning anything, and shutting her down if she dares to do so.

She's grateful that he does a lot of the cooking and cleaning, though. She can't quite get her head around how all the new appliances work. She thinks she, like everyone else, has too much time on her hands now. There are appliances for everything; no one cooks or cleans the old way. Timers switch everything on and off so they don't even have to do that.

Lori keeps insisting that they don't need all of this stuff and that they don't have to comply with every new rule set, but Elliot shakes his head at her and tells her she's talking nonsense. He's become one of them, like a Stepford husband, his thoughts no longer his own.

'The usual, honey?' he asks as he realises she's sitting behind him.

'Of course, what else?' she replies. She knows it's not really his fault, but she can't hold the bitterness inside sometimes. She immediately regrets it, though. She wishes he would snap out of this spell he seems to be under so that he wouldn't be so scared of breaking some rules every now and then. She knows he's noticed that her anger at all of it and at him for going along with it is getting worse. It's not like she's been subtle about it. She struggles to bite her tongue more and more as time goes on.

'You look nice today,' says Elliot in an attempt to smooth things over and maybe even get a smile out of her. She hasn't dressed up today in any way; she's wearing a pair of white jeans with a loose-fitted, lemon-coloured t-shirt and her white sports shoes. Her long blonde hair hangs loosely down her back. She's been told it should be tied back at all times for health and safety reasons, but she's not letting them win that one just yet. She tries to hang onto everything she can without breaking any laws.

'Thanks. I thought I might sit outside for a bit later and enjoy some sunshine. It's supposed to be a nice day for a change.' It comes out of her almost like a plea for him to say he'll join her.

'Maybe I'll join you,' he says, but they both know he won't. 'Don't forget not to stay out too long though. The sun will damage your skin, remember.'

Lori can't help but roll her eyes. He did actually venture outside this morning to take a few things from the house to store in the shed. She watched from the window as he stopped for a second, inhaling the fresh air deep into his lungs, as though he was trying to take in as much as he could before going back inside.

Lori looks around their pure white kitchen. Everything is such a bright white it gives her a headache sometimes; it's all pale and bland and often too bright for her eyes. Most houses look the same these days. It's supposed to promote well-being and calmness, or so they're told. There are so many rules to follow now if you want to live in a decent home, including the colour of everything and the appliances you must have to keep it clean and well-maintained. No one is allowed to be outside for more than an hour a day after the air became so polluted, it was considered a health hazard. All homes must have multiple air purifiers, which buzz loudly all day and night. You'd think they would have come up with a way to make quieter ones by now, with all the spare time everyone has.

It's the children Lori feels most sorry for. She can't imagine growing up without being able to go out with your friends to the park or riding bikes or climbing trees. Parks have been replaced with indoor gyms where children can go to get their exercise. The gyms are just the same as adult gyms, but with child-sized equipment. It's sad to know that they won't know what it's like to play sports outside where they can interact with other children, not even running around on the grass and just being silly. This is why Lori and Elliot decided not to have children, because Lori didn't want them to grow up in a world like this. She hopes one day things will change, but she can't see it happening any time soon.

Because of the severe health warnings, most people don't even want to spend an hour a day outside anymore. People have become so afraid and unsure of what is good and what is bad.

Lori's parents and brother are coming over later for an overnight visit. She can't wait to see them. They feel the same as her about everything and try to find ways around all the new laws, so they keep some aspects of their life as normal as possible. They managed to keep their house just outside of the city, where the laws are slower to be passed. Their area is next on the list to have all the new house laws enforced, but for now their house is still full of colour and character, or as full as it can be right now.

Lori knows Elliot hates that she doesn't agree with all this new technology and the laws surrounding it, but she likes to believe it's mostly because he doesn't want her to get into any trouble.

*

'Breakfast was lovely, thank you,' says Lori as she gets up from the island and puts her plate in the dishwasher. Elliot has finished his too and follows suit. Lori usually does this while Elliot checks that all their appliances and devices are charged or put on charge if they need to be. She can't stand how everything needs to be charged all the time and how much it messes up their day if they forget something.

'Let me put these in for you for a change today,' says Eliot, kissing Lori playfully on the nose.

'Okay,' she says, unable to stop the smile spreading across her face. He doesn't show his old self often anymore, so it's always nice when he does. She sits and watches him load the dishwasher and feels something similar to what she used to feel when she looked at him.

'When you've done that,' she says, 'do you fancy a dance with your wife if I put some music on?'

Elliot turns to face her with that old, familiar big smile, looking surprised.

'I guess I could,' he says.

She taps into her playlist and looks for an old one to play. She picks Long Live by Taylor Swift, and Elliot starts laughing.

'I thought you meant a slow dance,' he says.

'We can still hold hands,' replies Lori, standing up from her stool and holding her hands out to him.

Elliot joins her in the middle of the kitchen, and they hold hands and dance away to the music, moving around unsynchronised, Lori turning one way, Elliot trying to turn the other. Both are unable to control their giggles. It gets more random with each move they make, which only makes them laugh even more. They haven't danced together in so long it's like they've forgotten how to, but Lori doesn't mind. It's more fun this way. Elliot takes a step back, taking his phone out of his pocket and taking a photo of Lori, still unable to contain her laughter. As Lori catches sight of him doing this, taking a photo of her randomly because he wants to capture the moment, she again sees Elliot like he used to be and wishes she could hang on to this moment a little while longer.

But then the doorbell rings, and the moment is over, and Elliot snaps out of it.

'It's your parents,' he says. 'You'd better let them in.'

She knows moments like they've just had are rare now, so she goes over and kisses him on the cheek before answering the door.

'Thank you for that,' she says. 'I've missed this.'

He tries to hide it, but something in his eyes tells her he has too.

Lori always looks forward to seeing her family. There are big smiles and hugs all around when she opens the door.

'It's so good to see you all,' she says, leading them into the living room. 'So glad you can stay the night too. I dug out some old board games for us to play later.'

'I'm always happy to beat you at anything, sis,' says her younger brother, Liam.

'Haha, yes, that'll be the day,' she replies confidently.

'Behave, kids. We've only just walked through the door.

Thanks for paying for the travel, love,' their mother, Freya, says to Lori. They don't have as much money since her company made almost everyone redundant after switching to AI to do most roles instead. Now it's just Lori's dad, Alfie, working part time to pay the bills. Liam helps out with his job, but it's still only just enough.

'Anytime, Mam,' says Lori. 'You know I love having you all here.' Lori desperately misses going out for a coffee with her parents and taking walks in the park.

Elliot joins them, bringing in a trolley of hot drinks as they all take a seat. Elliot and Alfie always tend to drift to one side of the room discussing work and numbers. They're both accountants; one job that's still available, though opportunities are limited. Lori works as a travel agent, all online, of course. She finds herself glancing at Elliot every now and then and thinking about the connection they made earlier. She can't help smiling about it, but there's also a sadness that it might not happen again for a long time, if ever.

'You look well and happy,' says Freya, noticing the little smiles. 'How are you coping lately, being cooped indoors so much?'

Her mother knows she hates being in the house all day, especially in such a bland and boring house. Sitting at home all day booking flights and watching people get out of this country only deepens her hatred for where she is. Obviously, these laws are being adopted in most places, but some are still free, or freer than Lori is here at least.

'I'm okay, Mam. Still hating it, but I keep trying to find stuff to keep me occupied and pass the time. Work doesn't seem to take up much of my time lately. How are you? You look great too.'

'Thanks, I've been trying out these new skin products everyone's been raving about,' she says, turning her face side to side to give Lori a better look. 'They're supposed to reverse the ageing process.'

'Wow,' says Lori. 'Well, it seems to be working. Shame they can't reverse the time process and take us back to before.' She tries to laugh as if she's joking, but her mother knows her better than that.

'I know, love,' Freya replies, reaching her hand forward and placing it on Lori's. 'But let's not get all glum now. Did I tell you I found another set of books in the attic? Under the floorboards of all places. I thought one of them seemed loose, so your father took a look, and when he lifted it up, there they were.'

Freya always tries to keep things light, always trying to raise Lori's spirits in an attempt to distract her from feeling so trapped and confined.

They all spend a lovely evening together, playing card games and board games in front of the big, albeit fake, fireplace. They talk about anything and everything, like families do. This is the kind of thing that can't be taken away, no matter how hard the government might try.

They try to make the evening last as long as possible but resign themselves to bed when yawns spread around the room and eyelids start to become too heavy.

Everyone makes their way upstairs, and Lori makes sure her parents and brother have everything they need before saying goodnight.

'We have to leave early tomorrow, love, so I won't wake you up,' says Freya, leaning in for a tight hug. 'I've had a lovely time.' Her voice is soft and happy, and it fills Lori with a warm, loving feeling.

'Me too,' says Alfie, leaning over to wrap an arm around Lori and kissing her on the top of her head.

'Goodnight, everyone,' says Lori as they depart into their guest rooms, and she makes her way to her bedroom with Elliot. 'I'll see you soon, but I'll call you tomorrow anyway.'

She always has this yearning to tell them to take her back with them so she can escape this white prison, but she knows she couldn't leave Elliot. She knows he's still in there somewhere.

When she wakes in the morning and opens the blinds with her remote, the sun enters the bedroom like a welcome summer breeze, illuminating everything with an almost blinding glow.

She does a big stretch before getting out of bed and checks the time, wondering if it might still be early enough for her to say a quick goodbye to her family, but it's too late. She walks into the kitchen as Elliot is putting their coffee cups in the dishwasher.

'You just missed them,' he says, noticing the disappointment in her face. He hands her a cup of coffee, and she perches on the edge of a stool by the island, still not fully awake after jumping out of bed so quickly.

'I thought I'd treat them to a ride home in our helicopter,' says Elliot. 'They'll be home in no time.'

The mug of coffee slips right out of Lori's hand and crashes onto the floor, shattering into hundreds of tiny pieces. Her eyes are wide and filling with tears.

'What is it?' asks Elliot, panic rising in his voice.

'Did you charge the helicopter?' she asks, her voice barely above a whisper, already knowing the answer but hoping she's wrong.

Elliot's face drops and turns white, and she knows she's right. Instead of charging everything yesterday, Elliot was loading the dishwasher and dancing with Lori in the kitchen. They danced and laughed and forgot about everything else for a moment.

'Oh my god,' says Lori, and Elliot just holds her as best he can while her sobs echo through their home.

* * *

*

Lori locks herself in the bedroom for the rest of the day, refusing to come out for anything or to let Elliot in. For a while he sits on the floor by the door, listening to her crying and wondering how he could have possibly forgotten something so important. This is the first time he's allowed himself to feel the deep hatred Lori feels for the way things are. He let his guard down for one quick moment to enjoy a rare morning of humanity and laughter with his wife and look where it's gotten him. It shouldn't be like that.

Lori eventually leaves the room and walks lifelessly to the back garden, her face red and puffy and her body tired. Elliot stands in the doorway, watching the back of her head, trying to figure out if she wants him to join her or leave her alone.

'Is there anything I can do for you?' he asks sincerely, but it feels like a stupid question.

'Sit down with me, please,' she says quietly.

They sit there until the sun sets and it gets too cold to sit outside any longer. Elliot helps her inside, and she crawls back into bed and stays there just over a week.

*

A month has passed, and Lori spends most of her time lately clinging to the brooch her father gave her and staring at the painting from her mother. Sometimes she thinks she can hear a faint voice coming from it and wonders if she's losing her mind. Elliot tries to console her, but she knows he blames himself. She doesn't blame him though; she blames this weird and inhumane world they live in now. She hates it more than ever. Now she and Elliot have only each other.

The only good thing to come from this unnecessary tragedy is that Lori now spends a lot of time in her garden, watching the flowers her father helped to plant grow. Elliot spends more time outside too, helping her take care of their little garden and talking to her in the way he used to. It's changed everything. They can't prove it yet, but they suspect that something in those irritatingly noisy air purifiers is brainwashing them. Sedating their minds so that they freely go along with everything. It's the only thing that makes sense. Lori always spent more time outdoors, more than she was allowed, and now that Elliot joins her, she can see him starting to come back to life. He even found a way to disable the alarms on their windows so that they can open the back ones a little without alerting anyone, letting fresh air in all day and night. They just need to come up with a plan to prove it and let other people know. How long they'll survive after that, they don't know.

Lori's mother always used to say to her when she was little that 'fresh air will do you good'. That has never been more true than it is now.

They know that when they reveal the truth to the world, they'll have to leave this house and go into hiding somewhere. Lori is sad that she'll have to leave her garden and her painting behind. They are the only parts of this house that feel valuable to her. She doesn't know why, but she always felt like something was telling her to go outside when she looked at the painting. She thought maybe it was just the scene of the family playing on a beach that made her want to get out of the house, but now she's not so sure. Now she feels like it was trying to warn her somehow.

She finds herself looking at it often, trying to take in all the details of it, examining it bit by bit, the textures and colours. She doesn't want to forget any of it. It's the last thing she looks at before she leaves, and she swears she can hear a voice coming from it again, like someone is yelling from far away, but it's so far that she can't quite make out what they're saying. Each time she looks at it, she's convinced there's a little more damage to it every time, like small parts where the paint is fading or the canvas is beginning to tear. Even the painting doesn't want to be here anymore; she can feel it. Maybe she's imagining it all, convincing herself that it's her long-gone relative who once owned it, as though she's living inside it, an Eliza that Lori knew nothing about.

Lori and Elliot manage to make connections with someone from a community where people live in secret, away from the laws and eyes of those in power, a place where they are protected. It sounds like a perfect place for them to escape to after exposing their findings about the air purifiers.

When they arrive, they feel like they've stepped back in time, decades earlier when life was simpler and better. It's a small village hidden in the mountains where they grow their own food, and technology is limited to avoid anyone finding them. The community is small, but it continues to grow.

Their house is searched after they leave, and Clara's painting, along with their home, is demolished. Clara can now rest in peace, just like she wanted to.

As the men search the house before demolishing it, Clara hears a radio message come through to them. A cyberattack has taken down all AI sites, and they can't get anything back up and running. Everything is down. Her final vision is of Lori and Elliot sitting on some grass, happy and at peace. Even though Clara has tears in her eyes, she's smiling too.

Lori and Elliot soon get the news that AI has been hijacked all over the world and that people are starting to live freely in their homes again. As much as the people in power try to get it all back up and running, it keeps getting attacked, with no idea of who the culprit is. People are venturing back outside, cautiously and slowly, but they'll get there and realise everything has been a hoax to get them to live a certain way.

For the first time in a long time, Lori and Elliot discuss

their future with children in it. Their new home has a copy of the painting they owned, painted by Lori from the time she spent engraving it into her memory. It's not exactly the same, but it's close.

'If we have a baby girl one day, I'd like to name her Eliza,' she says.

Clara

Epilogue

Clara was ready to leave this world. She had been around for so long that she felt she had no strength to keep going. She lifted the part of the curse that wouldn't allow the painting to be destroyed. For a while, she hated herself for where she had ended up and for putting herself there. She had spent her life wallowing in bitterness and punishing innocent people, just because it made her feel good at the time. It ate away at her for so long.

The only grace she could allow herself was that she did good in the end. After a long time in Monica's attic, she realised that if she hadn't been around, Monica would have lost her life and Mia would have been without her mother for the rest of hers. Lizzy would have been tormented and most likely murdered by David. Sue may not have taken a chance on Jesse, and Beth and Luke could have had their cosy lives torn apart by the return of Beth's parents.

As much as she tried to remind herself of this, she still couldn't get the others out of her head. Rob, Charles, Emma, and others in between. It took her such a long time, but she learnt the hard way that a life of love, compassion, and helping others was far more fulfilling than the way she had previously lived.

By the time she got to Lori's, she was fatigued. She had seen so many good times, but so many bad times too. She was exhausted and ready to go. As the painting was hacked to pieces by men in uniforms, Clara was at peace. She was a child walking through a field with her parents; she was on the farm feeding and tending to her animals; she was a young woman battling against the wind when a kind stranger offered a helping hand; she was a bride in a beautiful dress, standing next to a man who couldn't take his adoring eyes off her. She thinks of her daughter and the beautiful family she created. She thinks of Lori, and how she got to spend her last few years at home.

Clara smiles as the world begins to darken until, finally, there is nothing.

Acknowledgements

I would, as always, like to thank my husband, Paul, for looking after me and keeping me sane while writing. A special thank you to my daughter, Jodie, for being my amazing editor and cover designer on this book, while also juggling a job and being a busy mam.

Thank you to all the wonderful supporters on Instagram. To all the fellow indie writers and supporters. I have discovered so many good writers this last year who deserve more recognition for their work. There are too many to name all but two in particular, Hayley Anderton, for all the hard work she does running events and promotions for indie writers, and Bethany Russo, for being such a great supporter to myself and all indie writers. I have read books by both and they are both very talented writers. Thank you in advance to anyone who reads this book and takes the time to leave a review.

Made in United States
Orlando, FL
10 December 2024